The

TRACEY

Fragments

The

TRACEY

Fragments

MAUREEN MEDVED

a spider line book

Published in 1998 by
House of Anansi Press Limited
34 Lesmill Road
Toronto, Ontario
M3B 2T6

Distributed in Canada by
General Distribution Services Limited
30 Lesmill Road, Toronto, ON, M3B 2T6
Tel. (416) 445-3333
Fax (416) 445-5967
E-mail: Customer.Service@ccmailgw.genpub.com

02 01 00 99 98   1 2 3 4 5

Canadian Cataloguing in Publication Data
Medved, Maureen
The Tracey fragments
"A spider line book".
ISBN 0-88784-624-6
I. Title.
PS8576.E35T72 1998   C813'.54   C98-930771-9
PR9199.3.M42T72 1998

Cover Design: Bill Douglas @ The Bang
Typeset by ECW Type & Art, Oakville, Ontario

Printed and bound in Canada
*House of Anansi Press gratefully acknowledges the Canada Council for the Arts
and the Ontario Arts Council for their support of our publishing program.*

The
TRACEY
Fragments

I'm so happy. Have an amazing life. Now I'm going to scratch my eyes out.

Think I'm funny? I'M AN EMERGENCY — sitting here, naked underneath the flowers on this scummy shower curtain.

IT'S NOT MY FAULT. My DNA's fucked. You can ask Dr. Heker. Or, at least you could have, a lifetime ago. She was my psychiatrist. The problem is congenital, I heard her say once. Behind the door. I think she was on the phone.

I'd also like to thank my parents. Their parents. God. My boyfriend. ESPECIALLY MY BOYFRIEND. When we met, the world got so clear you could hear a fork tinging against a glass in Mozambique. These days, my head could explode and I'd never even notice.

My name is Tracey Berkowitz. Fifteen. Just a normal girl who hates herself.

Nobody can do anything. I can't talk about any of it.

I can't talk to them. I'd never go back to those freaking retards. Remember in the news when two retards made a kid?

That was me.

Just kidding.

Nothing outside this grimy window.

For days, I've been on and off this plastic seat.

Wondering why.

The world sucks.

No matter how you cut the world.

And I haven't talked to anyone on this bus.

Till now.

I'm heading somewhere.

Here where I'm from is black and white. Black sky, white snow. In the spring, the snow melts into two rivers that cross in Blue Jay Park. What's left surrounds miles of wavy grain. Black-and-white cows blotch the plain. Farmhouses crumble to dust. Dust blows into the city and whirls on street corners like little tornadoes.

I had no choice about growing up here. I was a hothouse cauliflower. My parents grew me here against my will.

I knew I'd do better in the streets. Become a rock star. Maybe join a freak show, force-fed so I can become a fat lady.

Maybe in a few years they'd appreciate me. Maybe not.

Before I left, I had plans to form a metalcore band made of me — Estuary Palomino, my stage name — and my boyfriend. My boyfriend is gorgeous. Famous. Long hair. And sings.

What happened that day wasn't my boyfriend.

My boyfriend's name is Billy Speed. Nobody calls him that. Only I call him that. Because he is my boyfriend. His real name is Bernie Himelfarb. That means Bernie Blue Heavens.

Billy Speed isn't like everyone else. He foams. A Venus off the half-hell. He could have anyone. No one else even knows him.

It's probably obvious I've been around. And around.

Yes, Billy Speed touched me. This one time. When it happened. Nobody steams the way we steamed each other. All those hot and tiny vapours vibrated when we touched skin to skin.

The other day, something happened. Made my life pornographic.

The day it happened. At Blue Jay Park. Sonny. Billy Speed. It. It's not my fault.

When things happen, you come to certain realizations. I can't tell you what. You'll end up on this bus. Like me.

Looking for someone.

Sonny. That's my brother. My little doggie. Wish I had one of those whistles. He'd be here now. On the side of the road. Barking.

Before Sonny, I played every day by myself. Wrapped my legs around stalks of trees. Hoisted myself branch by branch till I forgot where I was. Squinted till my eyes became slits and the sky became sea. In the winter, I'd sit in snowbanks and pee if I had to. At night I pressed my face against my window screen. Mosquitoes whined and crickets whistled. I looked up at the stars.

Nobody knows how when Sonny came he made everything new.
   My father brought him to our house. Found him in the snow. My father told me. Under a dead bitch.

My parents didn't want Sonny.

Spoon in my mouth. Duck bib stretching out. Refrigerator humming. He grabbed her on his knee. She wriggled like she had to go to the bathroom. They fought like wild biting dogs, he leapt over her, turning, barking her all over the linoleum, sweat flying, chasing each other up the stairs and slamming the door. I heard them. Made the bed clack back and forth like a train on the tracks.

A head squeezed. Upsidedown between a pair of legs. Then a slippery elephant trunk. In that order.
   Sonny came out smirking, like he was born into a joke.
   "It was your fault," my mother said, glaring at my father from under her hair.
   "Sure, it was all my fault," he said.

I wanted Sonny. He was my baby. I fed him. I washed him with soap in the sink. I put him to bed in his crib.

Now I don't have anything. Except this hard plastic stuck all over me. Big ugly flowers. Shower-curtain ring-holes. My eyes in this dirty bus window.

And I don't care.

I'll stay on this bus till I find Sonny. I'll ride around in here, smearing the dirt from this window to see.

Sonny was ten. Yellow hair. Blue eyes flashing. Hoarse voice rubbing like sandpaper. Smirk twisting, like he knew he'd done something bad. HE DID DO SOMETHING BAD. It's all he ever did. Stuffed socks down the toilet to watch it explode. Lit lawns on fire. Stuck running hoses down basement windows. Covered himself in chocolate sauce and ran naked through the house. Pulled the In Case of Fire alarm. JUST TO SEE WHAT WOULD HAPPEN. Sonny never acted like a baby. Never cried. Never said You promised or I'm telling. He was ten. I was fifteen. He was my little brother.

"Are you keeping an eye on Sonny?" said my father, his voice repeating. Over and over like a car alarm.

Yes, I said inside my brain.

"Did you hear me?"

"Yes," I said out loud.

"You don't sound like you mean it. You really should say it like you mean it. If you do that enough, you'll believe it."

I told him I meant it, just to shut him up.

I DID MEAN IT.

Really.

Last year, when I was still a child, Sonny and I played every day in the field near Blue Jay Park. We weren't allowed inside. The water there's black and filled with gumboots, cans, and sludge. In winter, only the crows and certain revolting kids from my school stare out from the leaves. In summer, most of those park kids go on vacation. I'd sit with Sonny in the bushes. He'd fold his hand in mine and we'd watch the swans floating along the water like crumpled paper.

The swans are mainly white. Some are black. The black swans have ruby bills. I wouldn't know. I can't see colours. I'm colour blind. The experts don't agree. They say I've got concentration problems. What they're really saying is I'm stupid.

"We don't understand," said my teacher Mr. Sakamoto to my parents. "Perhaps Tracey would consider becoming a flight attendant. Yes, she'll serve people, but she'll get to fly in planes."

So what if I didn't colour in their maps of the world? They don't know how the knives in my skull carve tunnels to other places.

I sat at my school desk, folding the map over and over. Strangled out a neck. Crumpled it into the garbage.

The school fished the map out. My parents brought it home. Nerves shot against the walls. They flattened the map on the kitchen table. Veins running up and down the paper where I'd crumpled it.

"Another piece of evidence that you're standing out like bloody thumbs," my mother said. "You are forcing us to send you to a psychiatrist. Is that what you want?"

Sure, it's exactly what I'd always hoped for, right after turning my kidneys into earrings. I'd never in a million years go to a shrink. I'd have to be nuts.

"Dear," said Dr. Heker at our very first appointment. I hate when anyone calls me dear.

"Dear," she said again, just to get my goat. "Is there any reason you have chosen *not* to stay within the lines of the North American continent?"

I couldn't stay within the lines. I couldn't write properly, either. My mind is too small, I told her. She didn't understand, my mind was so small it flew outside the world to other more extraordinary places. It wasn't that I couldn't concentrate. I concentrated too hard. I concentrated so hard I made all the colours in the world fall down a black hole.

Seeds fall into holes. Seeds divide into good and bad.

"Good seeds sprout, bad seeds pout," my mother always said.

Bad seeds: Edi Amin, because he killed like trillions of people.

Jim Jones, because he invented that Kool-Aid acid cult. My grandmother, because she became a disgusting evil slut. Me, because my DNA takes after my grandmother's.

People, all the people I infect, because they are bad.

Good seeds: chrysanthemums, daffodils, tulips, roses, carnations, violets, lavenders, camomiles, mums, gladioli, begonias.

Flowers. Fuck.

Life goes in, life goes out.

I came from a hole. If you met my mother, you'd never believe that's where I'm from. She once pretended she loved me. Now she thinks my birth was a criminal act.

She's got this guy she's involved with. My father. If you met either one of them, you'd know I'm not the one who needs a shrink.

When I was a child, I would pretend I was blind. I'd feel my way along prickly bushes and tree bark tarred with sticky bands that kept the bugs away. I knew if I opened my eyes, even a sliver, God would strike me dead.

Once I grabbed a thorn. It pierced my skin. My eyes flashed open. The thorn speared my palm. Blood sprung out. I plucked a cherry from the thorny bush. Pressed it between my palms like a crow's heart. Smeared it on my legs.

One day, I made Sonny into a dog.

I hypnotized him. He barked like a dog. Flattened his palms. Arched his back. Growled. The mailman came. My mother opened the door. Sonny leapt out and barked him down the street. The mailman laughed till Sonny wrenched his pants between his teeth.

My parents got scared.

"Make him stop," my mother cried at me.

I couldn't get him to stop. I COULDN'T. I kept snapping my fingers in Sonny's face and told him he wasn't a dog any more.

Yes, I knew he wanted to touch me. And yes yes yes, I never asked him to stop touching me all over the place till it was too late for him to stop and I knew it was because he wanted to touch me and I wanted him to do it, too.

Billy Speed touched me on the street. In a tree. In Mozambique. WE EVEN WENT THERE ONCE. On a ship. One with pools and restaurants on different floors. We drank Cinzano. Because because because he is famous. I don't like to talk about it.

I have to be incognito.

Is it true, these seats kill?

I heard an expert say it on the news. The poly-something-or-other they're made from gives off a kind of poison gas. Do you think that's true because I've been sitting here a while.

We made the windows steam so bad you couldn't see. YOU COULDN'T EVEN SEE. One kiss wasn't enough. I had to put him in my mouth. I had to put him inside me where he can't get out.

That's what happens when you love someone. You want to fuck him all the time. You probably don't even know what I mean.

Everyone does it.

Fucks.

Except my parents. They did once. Twice. But my father must've fallen over my mother because they said we were accidents.

Even my teacher Mr. Sakamoto fucked Mrs. Sakamoto. She was the principal at our school. They barely said hello in the hall, but they fucked in Mrs. Sakamoto's office between classes. They did it on the desk. On the ink blotter. Mrs. Sakamoto put her calls on hold. She untied her hair. Mr. Sakamoto pulled open his zipper.

A pencil fell out.

Billy Speed carried me around at parties because I am small and delicate and it turned him into a gothrock hero.

This one time. He carried me. To the Mall Hotel and Bus Depot. We had to go. Because because because he had to meet this guy. His dad. Billy's dad drives the night bus to Fargo. And and and the whole way, I kept slipping and Billy Speed picked me out of the ice like a penny and said I love you like a million trillion times. Billy's dad put me on the bus away from Billy. Billy exploded his dad with a stick of dynamite.

Me and Billy were free and then we ran away.

Billy Speed bought me presents. Even this necklace with my name on. HE BOUGHT ME THAT. It was real expensive. Made from titanium. A million carats, or whatever.

It's somewhere.

Not here.

Must've got lost.

I'm getting out of here. This bus is full of criminals and thieves. Give me a cell phone. I want to call Billy Speed to come get me. It's one of the reasons I'm not in school. He was always interrupting the class. Not by knocking. He zoomed his Fat Boy right to the door of my classroom and revved his motor.

It was hard having two identities: normal teenager and biker bitch. I was tired of having to explain it, or whatever.

He wanted to buy me a motorcycle. It's the truth. Honest.

WHY WOULD I LIE?

Why do you think I'd sit on this bus?

Unless I absolutely had to.

I WOULDN'T.

Billy Speed doesn't really play in a band. HE COULD'VE. I'd go to every concert. I'd sit at the front. In the wings. I don't care. Because he is a star to me. He burns. Down the halls of the school. Down the halls of the mall.

He is the most gorgeous boy in the world. I've ever seen. In any music video. Anywhere.

Eyes the colour of the sky before it turns black. Hair the gnashing together of vines. He doesn't want just any girl.

He picked me.

When I got on this bus two days ago, I went straight to the back so the driver can't see I'm naked.

I take a different bus every night, depending on my mood. When I'm depressed, I like to be around other depressed people.

Depressed people make me happy.

"Are you happy?" Dr. Heker asked me one thousand times like I was a stone.

Happy?

Isn't it obvious?

My parents stood over me, buzzing. "Tell her," said my mother, first real quiet, then her voice got higher and higher. "Tell her you're happy, tell her you're happy," till it got so high it turned into the invisible whine of a missile arrowing towards the earth.

Happy people depress me. They're shiny. Their teeth knife so bright and white it's blinding. Look around you — there there there and there — happy people all over the place like an infection.

Sometimes I have to close my eyes around people like that. Sometimes I need to scream SHUT YOUR STUPID DAY-GLO MOUTHS before I stick you on the front of my bike and go night riding.

Murder. I think about murder a lot.

I have this medical condition. Makes me want to kill and fuck all the time. Lucky for us, it's in remission.

Sucks out loud, people not trusting me.

I wouldn't kill anyone. I just want to. Jealousy, hate, guilt, desire. Feelings. I want to murder people at least twice a day. But that's just a feeling. Dr. Heker said it's safe to have feelings.

"Can I feel like murder?"

"No problem, feel like killing anyone you want."

"Can I want to fuck my best friend's boyfriend?"

"It's only a want. Be my guest."

"Can I desire to throw myself out a moving vehicle when it's going ninety miles per hour?"

Desire. It's just a feeling. Nothing to be afraid of.

I just felt something. Now. Billy Speed. He touched my body with his fingers. Burned holes in my skin with his mouth.

Doing. That's different from feeling. Run, fall, drive, fuck. Doing something isn't safe. I don't know how anyone gets behind the wheel of a car. I won't drive. Not that they'd let me. I'm too young. But if I did I'd drive like at an arcade. I'd be all over, spinning the wheel like I was flying. I'd crack them in their heads and watch them break into a million pieces like the shell of an egg.

"Express your anger," Dr. Heker told me. "Let it out."

Maybe I'll express it.

My mother wouldn't make milk. One day, she dried up, splintered, and crumbled like bones.

I'm not angry, I told Dr. Heker. A TRILLION TIMES. Of course, I'm a liar and an exaggerator.

"You exaggerate," my father said. "I don't know what to believe and what not to believe."

It's hard to tell the difference between what's real and what's not when your whole life is inside your head. What's made up is usually better than what's real anyway. It's pretty much a no-brainer.

"Tracey," said Dr. Heker, "do you know I care about you?"

I knew the only thing she cared about for sure was the eighty bucks an hour they paid her so I didn't become a psycho.

Look at me.

It's too late for that.

"Tracey," she said, "as your psychiatrist —"

I don't know why she always said this. I think she, herself, was amazed sometimes that she was a psychiatrist.

"Tracey, as your psychiatrist, I am of the opinion that you might think you want to get better, but you don't really want to get better."

"I *do* want to get better."

"Then why are you resisting me?"

"I'm not resisting you."

"You're doing it right now."

"Tell me what to do."

"I can't tell you."

"Then how am I supposed to stop resisting you?"

"I can't tell you that."

"I CAN'T DISCUSS THIS ANY MORE."

"Can't is a choice."

"Okay, am I resisting you now?"

"Are you?"

This isn't an abuse story. I don't cry over spilt milk. I don't even drink milk. I'm lactose intolerant. I should've run away from home forty trillion years ago, but I wasn't abused.

Take my father.

You can say he's my father. He shot me into my mother.

My father doesn't work. Ever since my grandmother died,

my father had to stay home, so he could take care of my mother. He said he could no longer concentrate on trading futures.

"Don't cry for Daddy," my mother said. "He was never very good at stocks and bonds. Daddy missed the boat."

"Ha, ha, ha," said my father.

"You're the only one laughing," said my mother.

He ran around, screaming his head off.

"I've got a right to yell."

"Not if it breaks my eardrums," said my mother.

"Better your ears than my heart."

When he wasn't doing that, he read the papers. He even took them in the bathroom. He thought the bathroom was the only safe place in our house. You wouldn't want to touch those papers when he was finished. Not that I read the paper. It was hard for me to concentrate on the facts. So I didn't.

Don't get me started on my mother.

She wanted to kill me.

She tried to murder me with Velveeta. "I'M LACTOSE INTOLERANT," I screamed. She didn't listen. She said we must eat Velveeta. My grandmother, Baba, never drank milk, but never gave it either. When Baba got old she snapped in two.

We ate lumps melted on white bread that tore in the middle and looked like the paste from school.

My mother never ate with us. Just with the TV. Off a table with wheel feet. Red hair mangled on the pillow. Statue hands. Skin pouting like white bread between her pant seams.

"This wasn't in the stars for me," my mother said.

"What?" said my father.

"This," she screamed at the TV. "My life."

Ever since I shot out of my mother, I ruined her life. My mother won't talk to me. She's too busy. She smokes three packs a day and getting her away from the TV is a surgical procedure.

"I pierced my clit with a darning needle," I said one day.

She said nothing.

"I'm pregnant."
Nothing.
I told her I injected speed balls into my eyes.
Nothing. She just stared at the TV.
It wasn't even on.

I don't care.
I DON'T EVEN CARE.
Just waited for them to flare and burn themselves out like the pointed tips of the sun.

My father forgot.
It was his idea.
About Sonny being a dog.

When I was a baby, lying in my cot, my bedroom door cracked open. A piece of light ran across the floor like a mouse. First a nose, then the rest of my father came through the door.

"I just came to say goodnight." He stood by the door, looking like he forgot where he was. Walked over. Sat on the edge of my bed. The bed squeaked. My end went up.

"Sonny once had a mother who loved him very much," he said.

"Where was his father?"

"That's not the point," he said, voice razoring. "I went out with wild Eskimo hunters. Shot a dog."

"Did the dog die?"

He shook his glass. Stared into it. The ice chinked like wind-chimes we once had. "It died. Of course the mother of the baby died. We rolled her over. Found the baby underneath her body."

"A baby," I cried.

"Yes," he said like he was mad I interrupted. "A baby. Obviously we weren't going to kill the baby, so we strapped him onto the bobsled and brought him home to live with us."

Big silence.

We both stared at a crack in the floor.

"Sometimes." His voice cracked. Stopped and started like the frozen engine of a car. "Sometimes the baby cries for his mother whose blood can still be seen in the snow."

I knew he was lying. Sonny never cries.

My father's head dipped. Water fell down onto his housecoat. Made the colour dark. His fingers pressed into his eyes.

He looked younger than me when he cried. Younger than Sonny. I wanted to save him. I touched the belt of his housecoat with my fingers. "What's wrong, Daddy?"

He swallowed hard, looked up at the ceiling, eyes wet and gleaming. "I made up a part," he said. "She isn't really dead."

Next day, we visited Sonny's mother at the zoo. Wild dogs scrambling in a cage. Laughing their triangular heads off, white teeth pushing out like candy in a cake. Fur pieces, dust rising.

My father lifted me, hanging me over the bar.

"Which one?" I screamed.

"There she is. There's Sonny's mother," he said, pointing. "The bitch. The bitch. The bitch."

"Are you on drugs?" Dr. Heker asked me one day.

"OF COURSE NOT."

"What do you mean, of course not?"

"Don't you believe me?"

"I've been told that you're taking drugs." She read very carefully, scrunching her eyes into a file, bobbing her head like it was attached to a spring. "Your parents are concerned you're not paying attention. They think you're smoking crack."

PAY ATTENTION.

"My parents are lying."

"Come now, Tracey," she said, returning the letter to the file. "Your parents would have no reason to lie, would they?"

"How do I know what motivates my parents."

"I see. How can we continue our sessions together if you keep missing them and, possibly, taking addictive substances? It's obvious you are not serious about your recovery."

"I AM SO SERIOUS."

"It just so happens I believe you," she said. "I don't necessarily agree with your parents that you need to see me."

I told her I didn't care.

I didn't.

Around me, people always breathe through their mouths. It's not my fault I smell like a sewer crocodile.

Things aren't as bad as they seem.

They're worse.

This year I flunked school. It wasn't a priority any more. I told Dr. Heker. She didn't agree with me.

"As your psychiatrist, I cannot agree with you, Tracey."

My parents wanted me to do something with my life.

I did something.

Now I ride around on buses.

Every year I got something more wrong with me. My parents' eyes burned me around the house, trying to figure out what.

"You're a late developer," my father said once over dinner, pointing at me with the knife he used to cut his meat. "It's normal," he said. "Don't worry about it."

I didn't worry about it until he mentioned it.

AFTER THAT, IT WAS ALL I WORRIED ABOUT.

Sure, I ran away. It was like living with a pair of Helen Kellers. All they did was feel.

One day I ran through the snow. I ran and ran until I ran all the way back home. My father was in the kitchen, newspapers crumpling, socks rubbing together under the kitchen table. This woman, my mother, was on the sofa downstairs, cigarette in one hand, TV remote in the other. I knew she heard me come in because she turned up the volume on a screechy, shrieky gameshow voice.

My parents had this problem about me going outside. They thought I was going to get murdered every time I left the house.

"Shut the door, please," my father shouted from the kitchen.

They also had this problem about the door. They made me lock the door when I came in, before I went to bed, before I took my boots off. Because of my grandmother. Because her DNA, or whatever, made our lives unravel and tangle up like a yo-yo string.

"You're just like Baba," my father said.

My parents refused to come downstairs unless we locked the door. All the way.

Once, Sonny left the door wide open. JUST TO SEE WHAT WOULD HAPPEN. It slapped the frame and rushed my parents to their bed.

"Is the door locked?" my father asked me.

I leaned against it. Clicked it into place. I heard my father on the stairs, socks shuffling on the last step.

I told him, it's locked.

He curled his head around the corner like he didn't believe me. Because I exaggerate. OF COURSE I EXAGGERATE.

It's not my fault.

I couldn't think in that environment.

My father leaned over the last step, socks muffling. "You've got to pay attention," he said. "If you pay attention, you won't forget to lock the door."

PAY ATTENTION. PAY ATTENTION. PAY ATTENTION.

"Where's your head?" he asked me.

UP YOUR HAIRY ASS, I wanted to scream.

The words came out of his mouth. IT WAS REALLY HER. On the sofa. Didn't speak. Threw her voice. Hole in his back she stuck her hand through. Made his mouth jump up and down.

"Did you lock it?"

"Yes."

"I'm warning you."

I wanted to cut him into pieces. Feed him to the squirrels.

"I told you."

"All the way?"

• 24

He peered to see it was locked all the way, then stepped down and stood in the hall with newspapers bunched in his hand. He had to check to make sure I REALLY did it. His bathrobe was loose. Undershirt stuck out. Coffee stains. White marks jagged around his calves where the socks fell.

"You disobeyed us," he said.

I couldn't argue with the facts.

"Do you have any idea what time it is?"

I stood there in my parka, the snow melting on the floor. "I guess I'll go to my room," I said.

"Not so fast," he said. "Where were you?"

I didn't look at him. "No place. Stuff's bugging me," was all I could think to say.

Something you should know about my father is he hates slang. He associates slang with degenerates. He stared at me like he could open my mind. I didn't know what he wanted to hear, so I told him everything bugs me. BUGS ME. I made sure to say it twice.

He squeezed the papers with his fist, then he turned to my mother and asked her to turn off the TV, please. He was scared of her. She knew it. She lifted the remote and changed the channel.

"Turn it off," he said, a little louder, slapping the papers hard against his leg. "We've got a crisis."

She increased the volume.

"We've got a FUCKING crisis," he shouted.

She clicked off the remote, then went upstairs to their room and shut the door.

He watched her go, then turned to me. "You're grounded."

And I was.

For years.

"WHAT?" I screamed. "AGAIN?"

Stuck with them in the house.

I'd slit my wrists.

My father followed my mother up the stairs.

My parka whined as I slid along the wall. That sound. I hate it. HATE IT.

Something you should know, I'm extremely sensitive to sounds. I can hear EVERYTHING. I can hear bones shrinking. The way my grandmother's did till she died.

I sat on the floor. My father clicked open the door to their bedroom. He asked my mother what's going on.

She didn't answer. The mattress springs squeezed together. Their feet squeaked the floor above my head. He asked her again. This time his voice made a tiny pleading sound. She told him to leave her alone. He said something I couldn't hear. Then something heavy thudded to the floor. Sometimes she does that, falls onto the floor. I saw her do it once. She cried so hard, foam came out of her mouth.

When a horse falls, foam comes out of its mouth. When it falls, the legs of the horse thrash and the horse is no good, so somebody shoots the horse. The horse turns into glue. A machine puts the glue into bottles. Some of the bottles have nipples and children squeeze the nipples to get the glue out and stick bits of paper onto cards. Glue gets on the children's hands and the children eat the glue. The children become the horse.

I'm a horse. The horse the man road away with Baba on.

I am a very passionate person. I was born to love, no matter what.

Just look at me, sitting here, naked on this bus.

Love pumps though my blood. Not from my parents. In our family, passion's like diabetes — it skips a generation.

Even though my grandmother's dead, she tells me these stories, buzzing my DNA like a radio caught between the stations.

The parents of my grandparents. They were born into poverty. Their parents were also dirt poor. Like every generation before them. My whole family — all the way back to when the earth was ruled by amoebas — were slaves, serfs, losers, thieves.

In Balilfka, the little Polish village where my grandmother's from, everyone slept in one bed. Icicles drove against her in the night — long, white, dripping, soaking the back of Baba's nightdress. She didn't fuck — she was only fifteen — but she thought about it. She couldn't help it. She shared the bedroom with farm animals. She saw them stuck together. Vibrating. Smaller versions of the same animals fell out of holes.

Baba gangled through the high fields. She wasn't a beauty. She had a moustache and no tits. She had dark eyes and full, red lips, though. She wasn't smart. Never asked questions. If she asked a single question, she'd get killed. She had curiosity, though. Her eyes darted. She sniffed around. Tried to pick up why everyone in town hated her family. But because she was the oldest girl, Baba's job was to be a slave. She babysat. Scrubbed pots. Peeled potatoes. Cleaned the herring fish.

A piece of herring can't love.

When she was lonely, Baba cuddled the corners, watching the cats jump. Whenever she could, she ran up and down the yard. Cows mooed. Chickens jerked. Birds skittered the skies and flung themselves from branch to naked branch. She rolled up and down the little hills, collecting dandelion fluff in the lining of her dress. When she ran too far, her mother caught her by the ear.

"Keep the door closed. Always, the door must be closed. Here on this land sits our house. Outside the house there are Jews. Outside the Jews there are Gentiles. Outside the Gentiles there are men on horseback, their hearts as black as crows."

While she scrubbed the pots, Baba daydreamed about those men — hoofs pounding up through the grass, dust whipping under the hoofs, whipping up, clouding the men into ghosts. They lifted themselves above her by their thick, sinewy arms. She was so small, Baba rolled under and away from the men through the tall grasses. The men rolled after her, tearing out the front of her dress, biting her nipples between their teeth. The heat of the dust rose up between her legs. Her body shuddered so hard she had to lean against a tree. At night, the lungs of family and farm animals beat steadily around her until they almost swallowed Baba. She cried for something to happen — anything — to change her mind.

One day something happened.

Baba carried plates from the table to the kitchen. From the kitchen to the table. Mouths spitting and oozing meat shouted. Orders rose around her like horse dust. She got fed up. Refused to carry soup to the men at the table. The hunger inside her had to be filled. Everyone yelled. Yanked her hair. Slapped her around. Baba spun, smaller and smaller until nobody could see her. She slipped through a crack in the barn floor. Under the wooden slats, my grandmother held her heart, a bird, wildly flapping.

Heads bowed in prayer.

Night bled from the sky.

Hoofs thundered. Cracked the night in two. Baba's heart shot her straight through the slats. The pounding neared. She edged to the door. Light flashed through a crack. She edged the door open with her fingers. The door banged hard against the wall, and a group of men on horseback burst inside.

One of the men was beautiful — long red hair, thigh muscles rubbing against his horse. Baba gazed at the horseman. She dreamed she was the horse and the man would ride her away, feed her sugar, and brush her hair. The horseman scooped Baba up. He whipped her away on his horse down the little hills, near the stream that gurgled at the bottom.

At the bottom of the hill, the horseman threw Baba from his horse. She thudded to the ground. Over the fields, she heard her mother's shrieks tearing from the windows. Guns shot. Flames crackled and shrunk her house away. The horseman slammed Baba against a tree and slammed into her. Something cracked open. Blood spilled out. Baba's body shook, then went still.

Baba's horseman galloped away.

She flung herself into the stream and sat in the muddy water for days, throat swollen, unable to cry.

They wouldn't let me out of the house.

Not on school nights. Not any night. NOT EVER. PERIOD.

"God, God, God," cried my mother.

"Raped. Murdered. Is that what you want?" cried my father.

How am I supposed to answer that? Does that deserve an answer? But they expected one. So, I answered, "Yes."

"Yes, what?"

"Yes to rape. Yes to murder."

It had to be better than answering their stupid questions.

Grounded.

"It wouldn't kill you to stay inside," my father said.

"IT WOULD," I said.

Grounded.

"It makes us nervous. Can you grasp that?"

"Why?"

"Why doesn't matter."

I'm not here. I'm never here. I'm Estuary Palomino. Palomino, the white on white of the people who made me.

"What do we do with her?" my mother said, picking her hands, voice thinning out like a strangle.

Made me remember something my psychiatrist said. "Sounds like you've got some work to do," I said.

Grounded.

I couldn't stay there with them. In that house. And babysitting. And watching them watch TV.

They whirled in my head like torments.

They had the worst kitchen table habits in the human race. They should live behind zoo bars. Nose hairs moved when they breathed. Dressed like hospital patients. Made grunting, chewing, animal noises. I clapped my hands over my ears. Stared at my plate. Concentrated to make them disappear. I couldn't sit there any more without wanting to murder them in their beds.

I knew one day, they'd wake up and I'd be gone. It's all I thought about.

I had to escape. Because I didn't even care, or whatever. Because I thought I could get out and see the universe, which a person like me deserved. Because it was obvious to anyone with a brain and two eyes that a person like me either went to hell in a scary monster house or became a star and there's no in between.

Read the magazines. It's in there.

So, this week, Sonny and me smuggled out.

This one time.

When it happened.

Where? Where the sky splits from the world.

IT WAS THEIR FAULT. They never should have grounded me.

The day Sonny disappeared. They asked me what I'd done. If they knew. They can't ever know.

We all looked for Sonny. For two days. He never came back.

I slunk through the house. Concentrated really hard to disappear. It worked. Two days. Nobody talked to me.

They knew.

"Why don't you eat with us?" said my father. He looked up from his dish at my mother.

My mother stood there. Glared at me. Stepped into the hall, stretchy pants crying whenever her legs rubbed together.

I knew she blamed me.

"YOU THINK I DON'T KNOW WHAT YOU'RE DOING. I KNOW WHAT YOU ARE DOING. YOU ARE JUST SOME UGLY STUPID BITCH DYKE," I screamed.

Just kidding.

But I'd like to have said that.

What did I do? I lifted my bowl. Walked to the kitchen door. Spilled my dinner into the plastic bag hanging on the door knob.

What did she do? She came back into the kitchen. Pretended to ignore me. Acted like nothing was going on. Took a cigarette. Lit it. Exhaled till the smoke hid her eyes.

I thought, good, the bitch can't see me.

She waved the smoke away with her hand. Stared through me like she was watching TV on the other side of my head.

Dr. Heker gave me a crayon. "Why don't you draw what you're thinking right now," she said.

I ground that crayon between my teeth.

She rolled up in her chair. "Do you think you're creative?"

Guns go off. People have sex. People shoot up. People die. PEOPLE ACTUALLY DIE.

"Do you think you're creative?"

I think Dr. Heker was a little scared of me. I can tell when people are scared of me. They never look me in the eyes. My eyes narrow to slits that can burn holes.

"Do you think you're creative?"

I'd heard it a million times. From my parents.

My parents hated creative people. They hated artists. Artists kill presidents. Artists are freaks — losers, homosexuals, freaks, losers, communists, losers, poor, hungry, unloved, old, impoverished, young, hated, rich, immature, freaks, losers, pedophiles, sex fiends, undeveloped, impotent, womanizers, nymphos, sluts, losers.

"Do you think you're creative?"

The way my father crumpled the newspaper, rubbed his socks together under the table. The way my mother blew smoke from the hole in the middle of her face. The squeaky plates. Knives. Forks. Tinging. Tinging. Tinging till I thought I'd cut them up with those knives and turned them into holes.

That's what I did before I ran away.

Just kidding.

But I'll never go back.

I've got this theory. It's called the Reinvention Theory. This is how it goes. If you become somebody beat or fucked up then you will be unrecognizable to your parents and loved ones. They will beg you to change, but when they see you are a genuinely different person — because maybe you've dyed your hair seven different colours or obtained your allowance from dirty-fingered old men in the street or put a ring through your pussy or tattooed milk fucking toast on your forehead or scarred your body on all the visible areas or yelled words like shit cunt pussy dyke faggot mail-order bride, snuff flicks cock ring John Holmes is my Dad or cut off your body parts and mailed them care of Mom and Dad — then they'll realize how terribly sorry they are and they will kill themselves and leave you all their money and a blackboard with I fucked your life written two million times in their own blood.

I think about going back sometimes. I'll pretend to sell Jesus or some kind of magazine. They won't open the door, so I'll have to sneak my way through the radiator vents. My father will still be there with his newspaper, never changing out of that housecoat, my mother still clicking the remote, even after the batteries run out.

They won't ever forget.

I ran to the door and looked up at the sky. The wind outside was fierce. It whipped. Put holes in your body. Hung you upside down.

Sometimes you just have to do something.

It was easy. I opened the door. I closed the door.

Know the best part? My house shrinking away behind me.

I only had a bus pass and ten dollars and eighty-seven cents I'd stolen from my mother's purse that I kept in a plastic bag. I ran into the street. I looked back. My house, a dot.

Snow, street, bus, snow, street, bus.
   That's my life now.
   Two days. Maybe three. Can't remember.
   It's hard to see with the sun going down, swelling your eyes, pointy tips touching the edge of the world.
   The colour of the sky before it turns black.
   I can't believe people live out here. Miles of nothing but snow.

I don't like the country. Creeps me out. In the country, dead bodies lie in swamps, ditches, shallow graves. A man dumps the body of a girl in a ditch. The body rots and melts into slime. Flowers pop up where the body lies. Seeds fly out of the flowers. A bee sucks the flowers and makes honey. The family of the girl buys the honey from the store. The family eats the girl.
   Sonny —
   I'll find him standing by one of those all-night donut shops. With jam in his smirk.
   The park. Billy Speed. Then Sonny was gone.

A blizzard was about to hit. Newspapers screamed it from their boxes. People ran back and forth. Buses trudged between ice piled high like mountains.
   I got on. The bus pulled away.
   You can sleep on the bus. Better than a house. If you don't like where you are, you take a different bus. You don't pay rent.
   Look at me. I ride the bus and the bus and the bus. In circles. I don't care how many times.

Nobody can stop me.

You can't just lose your own little brother.

I couldn't sleep. I rode around. I didn't know where. I thought I'd stay on until I figured out what to do.

I watched things outside the window. It was like TV.

I watched the black river. Looked up at the black sky. Every other thing was white. The blizzard hadn't started. It was coming. Even the crows knew. Black wings thrashed. A bridge flew above me. I thought about going to visit Dr. Heker. My next appointment wasn't for two weeks. But it was all I could think about for some reason.

Dr. Heker worked downtown in a tall skinny building. I went straight up to her office. I didn't even knock. From behind her desk, she told me come back when it's time for your appointment. I stood there, clicking the door where it went in the wall. Her mouth went into a straight line. Made me so nervous, I sat in the chair. The one for patients. It was hard like an airport seat. Only in airports you're going someplace. In a psychiatrist's office, you're not going anyplace. Even if you need to go to the bathroom, they accuse you of being in resistance when you only need to pee.

Heker's eyes kept flicking down at the gold clock on her desk. She kept sighing, too. Her dirty breath blew everything around.

"There's a blizzard brewing," she said. "I'll be closing my office and going home myself after my next appointment."

I wondered where she went when she went home. I imagined she went to a condominium and drank Cinzano.

"Do you live in a condominium?" I said.

"A house," she said like a countertop. She wasn't too enthusiastic for someone who got paid a lot to see me.

"How many people live in your house?" I said. I was bouncing on the cushion of my chair that was made out of some kind of edible oil product. I suddenly got this brilliant idea. "I've got this idea," I said. "Maybe you can rent me a room."

Her eyes narrowed. She leaned over in her chair and clasped her hands. "Dear," she said, "I have a client coming."

That dear didn't get past me. I chose to ignore it.

"Maybe you'd like the company," I said.

"Let's discuss this at our appointment." She scribbled. I tried to see, but she curled her hand over it.

"You'd have someone there when you get home from work."

"You cannot move in with me."

"Why not?"

"Well, for one thing, there are certain rules."

"I won't tell anyone."

"Why aren't you at home with your family?"

"Because I'm insane. You know what that means?"

"Well, not exactly."

That surprised me a little.

"I should be locked up," I told her.

"That's something we can discuss at your next appointment."

"I don't know if I can wait."

"Go home, Tracey."

"What if I'm insane? I can't go there if I'm insane."

"You can talk to your parents about how you're feeling."

"Fuck that." I said it very quietly, so she didn't hear.

"What was that?"

"Nothing," I said.

"You've got to go, Tracey."

"I'm worried that I'm insane."

"If you're that worried, you can go to the hospital."

"Where they put the nutbars?"

"If you will."

"Will you come visit me?"

She stopped like she needed to think about it.

"Of course."

"How long will I stay? Will I be locked up forever? Like jail?"

"They'll probably evaluate you and let you go that same day."

I didn't say anything for a while. I wanted to go to the hospital, somewhere, anywhere, to get away. I needed a vacation.

"You might contact my secretary," she said. "If there is a cancellation, perhaps we can fit you in early next week."

Then, as I watched her babble, this terrible thought struck.

"Will they give me shock treatments? If they can't find my specific problem, or whatever?"

"What?"

"Electricity up and down your body. Like in Frankenstein. Blasts your brain wide open like a super-highway, so everything bad falls out. I read it in a magazine."

"What magazine?"

"It doesn't matter, but they said they can do it. Promise me you won't let them. Because I can't forget. I CAN'T FORGET ANYTHING."

"Forget what, dear?"

"You know what I'm talking about. You can see in my brain. That's why they pay you the big bucks."

"Sometimes it's better to just have fun and stop thinking so much. Sometimes we think too much, dear. Meanwhile, go home. Watch TV. Call your friends."

Just then I hated her. She couldn't see. ANYTHING. If I was a horse, she'd give me away. She'd shoot me. She'd turn me into glue.

She stared at her desk and took a deep breath.

That bugged me. BUGGED ME. Worse than the dears. Worse than anything. So what I did was, I tapped my boot against the foot of my chair. I tapped harder and harder until my chair rocked back and forth. She didn't even look at me. She looked at her watch, at the door. She looked mad. I wanted to burn down cities. Scream so loud it filled the galaxy. Snap the points off mountains and cut myself with those points and streak the sky with blood.

But I didn't.

It wasn't appropriate.

I bounced around in my chair, pretending that I wore a strait-jacket and all I could do was bounce around in my chair because I couldn't help myself because I was a maniac. A total maniac. I bounced around the whole room, because my hands were locked behind my back in this white jacket and nobody was there. It was just me and four white walls. A life sentence. In this little ugly white room. I went bang! bang! bang! BANG! around the room in this chair I had to sit in as a punishment for my maniac crimes.

Dr. Heker didn't even look at me.

"I want you to take a breath before you leave here," she said.

"I don't want to take a breath. Why don't YOU take a breath."

She sucked on the tip of her pen. Puckered tiny lips. Two petals of the same dead rose. I wanted to take an iron. Steam those lips shut. She pulled the pen out. Pointed it at me. "Do you believe I am responsible for your recovery?"

I told her I didn't know. I didn't. I seriously didn't know what the fuck she was talking about.

"You are the one who is responsible for your recovery," she said. "I could leave tomorrow and another therapist could take my place."

"WHAT other therapist?"

"There is no other therapist," she said. "I just want you to understand that your recovery is, ultimately, your responsibility."

Then I said the only thing I could think of. "I could clean the house while you're at work and when you get home maybe we could sit by the fire and have a little chat."

Then she stood up, looking angry and confused. "You're going to have to leave," she said. "Or I'm going to have to call your parents. Would you like me to call them?"

"Are you going to stop seeing me?"

"I never said that."

"Yes you did," I told her. "You absolutely did." I tried to remember. "Something about another therapist."

"I did not say I would stop seeing you."

"I'll leave first. You'll see."

"Should you choose to see another therapist — and that is absolutely your prerogative — we shall have to discuss that at your appointment. Would you like to make an appointment?"

"I'VE GOT AN APPOINTMENT," I screamed.

She looked a little frightened. "Well, I'm sorry," she said, and just the way she said it I knew she wasn't sorry. She liked saying it, not because she believed it was right, but because she was a stupid dumb coward and she sucked and I hated her and I could've strangled her with my hands and slipped out the window like a cat. Nobody would've known.

"I've really let this go on far longer than is appropriate," she said. "Now I have another client waiting outside."

"Of course you have another fucking client waiting outside."

"What did you say?"

"Nothing. I'm just kidding."

"It's okay to express your anger."

"What the fuck do you know?"

"I don't know, dear," she said. "Tell me."

"CUNT." Once I said it I couldn't stop. I must've said it forty times. I couldn't even believe it came out.

Her eyes goggled. They seriously did. She went to open the door to the waiting room. I went to take a look. A man with a bald head sat there with big broken eyes like the clocks at my school.

"I'm sorry," I said, and my voice trembled because I was very very scared. "I'd like to leave, but I can't until I know right now if you're going to send me to another psychiatrist."

"That was never my intention," she said, voice arcing like a plane in the sky.

"IT WAS," I screamed. "YOU'RE LYING. WHY WOULD I WANT TO SEE A PSYCHIATRIST WHO'S A BIG FAT LIAR, ANYWAY?"

"Perhaps if you wish to see someone else, you could discuss that with your parents. I'll confer with them myself."

She stared at me. I wanted to cry. I'd never do it in there. I made a sound, like I might have something to say. I did have things to say. I couldn't say them out loud. My mind went as black as the sky. I watched the snow fall against the glass. I watched the lights of the city light up the sky like stars.

I stood in the parking lot. Dinnertime. Nobody on the streets. People stuck inside with their families, killing each other. Most of the cars had gone home. The rest were plugged into sockets, still and steaming like lonely cows. A few people sat in trucks and cars, heating up their engines. Somebody scraped ice off a window.

One of the cars was Heker's. I wasn't absolutely sure which one. I thought seriously about kicking in some doors, but as I walked and walked, my feet grew heavy. All I saw in front of me were the sky and snow for miles. I was on the moon. I couldn't move because the gravitational force might pull me away.

I walked very hard and very fast and it didn't matter that I wasn't going home ever again as long as I live and it didn't matter that I had no money except for ten dollars and eighty-seven cents and it didn't matter that it was forty degrees below zero, everything frozen white — even the trees — because I was happy. I was absolutely fucking happy. I'd never been so fucking happy in my whole life.

The Pony Corral was practically the only real restaurant my family ever went to. It was just down our street. The waitresses wore brown and white checked uniforms. They brought a basket of handi-wipes smelling like lemons to your table. Next to the bathrooms there were a stable and pictures of famous horses.

The Pony Corral shut down and moved away. My father didn't want to drive there. "It's too far now," he said. After that we went to IHOP. I wanted to go to IHOP because it was new. Sonny refused to go. He liked the Pony Corral. He was crazy about horses. Dreamed he was a dog, riding a horse. Because he didn't have a horse, he turned his bed into a horse. He sat on top all day sometimes, yelling for his bed to go faster. He even stole my horse quilt from my bed. There were pictures of horses. Horseshoes. Cowgirls jumping. It always ended up on his bed, which was a horse anyway. He always broke through my bedroom door. Even if I locked the door, he picked the lock. When I went to his room to get my quilt, Sonny'd just bark and lope out the door.

This is the story of the girl with no tits.

This girl. Went to my school. No tits. Big dumb moon face. Slunk in wall creases. Sat at the back of the class. Folded up inside a book like one of those flowers when it pops from a hole.

Came from an expensive part of town. Not the most expensive. Not Tuxedo Heights. Next to it. The one for people almost as rich as the people in Tuxedo Heights. Attached garage. Family room. Heated terrarium. Where the flowers lived. Chesterfields covered in plastic. Sheets folded back sharp like paper cuts.

A scary monster house filled with a scary monster family. People still went there on Halloween.

Mommy and Daddy looked normal to the outside eye. They wore regular civilian clothes. They went to stores. They smiled. They said yes and thank you and you're welcome. The government allowed them to carry credit cards and cheque books.

Only the girl and her dog knew the truth.

Mommy and Daddy were really extras in a horror movie. The horror movie took place in a POW camp. And you can't escape that POW camp because you've been brainwashed. And your captors are not just monsters but evil bloodsucking aliens. And those aliens are from Russia — before Russia became our friends, or whatever.

Ever since the girl crawled out from Mommy's hole, Mommy crawled back inside her garden where flowers grow. Tucked around in her flower bed. Wiggled her fingers in the mud. Shook the package. Made a noise. Put the seeds in. Flowers sprung.

She sang to the flowers with her mouth. Cupped the blossoms with her hands. Hunks of mud clotted their hanging hairy roots.

Weeds is better cause weeds don't stink.

Sonny and It sat in weeds. Dandelions popping out of holes like little suns. Milked the stems. Fed stem into stem. Made necklaces.

It couldn't even see the colours of those flowers.

Mommy crouched in her garden, digging, purring, whispering, cupping her hands around the blossoms.

THE ONLY TIME SHE CUPPED THOSE STATUE HANDS AROUND ANYTHING.

"They're gorgeous. Look at the colours." She didn't even look at the girl when she said that.

That's because It looked like a boy. A long boy stretched out with a vagina. Not like a flower. Like mud. Skinny and gangling like sticks. Only worse, cause sticks is sharp.

"I can't even see the colours," the titless girl told her.

It couldn't. Really.

"You can see them," she said. "You just don't want to see them. Red begonias, pink cyclamens, purple lilacs, yellow daisies." She just went on and on and on and on till It wanted to yank those blossoms from their holes and shove them down her throat.

"I CAN'T SEE THEM," It screamed Its head off.

"You don't expect me to believe you can't see these colours," she said. "You're too smart for that. You're pretending."

"I'm not."

"That's just it," Mommy said. "The final piece of evidence we need to send you to a psychiatrist."

Behind It, Sonny scraped out a laugh.

Pouting pink lips. Blinking purple eyes. Tiny white fists. It learned the flowers anyway. By the shapes of their blossoms. Shades of grey. Shades of black. It memorized everything.

Even the blotchy flowers on this stupid shower curtain.

Not like Sonny's eyes. The same as Billy Speed's. Blue like the sky before it turns black. Dark — not too dark. Brown and red come out black. Blue is different. Flicks light out.

That night, Sonny barked down the stairs. He trampled Mommy's garden, smashing the flowers under his hands and knees.

"Stop it stop it stop it." Daddy wagged his finger in Sonny's face, looking confused and angry like when he tried to figure out the VCR. "You are not a dog."

But he was a dog.

A tiny plush dog with a black eye and velvet nose.

They never knew if the experiment was a success, or he was just playing along.

"You're supposed to take care of your little brother," Daddy said. "Not turn him into a dog."

Mommy and Daddy blamed It. OF COURSE THEY BLAMED IT.

"I'm holding you personally responsible," Daddy shouted, cringing the girl with no tits into a corner.

PERSONALLY PERSONALLY PERSONALLY RESPON- SIBLE.

Daddy whipped his belt from the loops. Snapped It up the stairs. Cracked It against the wall until stars blinked and danced.

It deserved it.

Mommy and Daddy REALLY REALLY REALLY wanted the girl with no tits to behave. All It ever did was behave. IT'S ALL IT EVER FUCKING DID. School, home, study, TV, bed, school, home, study, TV, bed. At night, swinging alone in Its empty room. Talking to Itself. Staring out windows. Sick of seeing just Its own face staring back.

The girl with no tits didn't fit into a group. Even the rejects. Over lunch, It stayed in the library. In home room. When It went anywhere, It went alone. When It crept against school walls, people held their breath. Careful to avoid direct skin contact so they didn't catch anything. Boys pulled at It. Blew their snot on It. Yelled, "It's coming." Lined up down the hall. Pressed sticks into It. Excited to see It squirm and dance.

One day, Mommy's Mommy came for a visit. Nobody but Mommy knew she had a Mommy. Not even Daddy.

"I can't stand it," Mommy said, flipping from the sink.

Nobody let Mommy's Mommy in the house.

Daddy cracked the door open, so all It saw was the gnarled

branch of a hand sticking through. "She doesn't want to see you," Daddy said in a low voice like very late at night.

Later that night, Daddy talked to Mommy in a whisper.

"She says she has cancer," Daddy said.

"That's what she says."

"She doesn't have much longer."

"Did she say that?"

"I'm assuming."

"Well, there's something to look forward to."

After that, Mommy told Daddy a scary story. Daddy told the same scary story to the girl with no tits. Night after night, stories twisted and twangled like the bedsheets between Daddy's fingers as the titless girl fell into Its dreams.

Every week, Mommy's Mommy left cakes. She brought them on the bus. Left them on the porch. Nobody took the cakes inside. They sat there until Mommy yelled at Daddy to take them away. He carried them in his arms like little babies to the garbage.

One day, Mommy's Mommy died. And Mommy went scared and mental and the flowers curled, shrivelled, and fell on the floor. Mommy crawled into the TV set. Wouldn't come out.

"Are you planning to do the dishes during this lifetime?" my father asked my mother in a teeny tiny baby voice.

My mother piled up the dishes in the laundry basket. Put them in the washing machine. Made a noise like a million cats dying.

My father ran over. Opened the washing machine door. Glass poured out. He warned us back with his hands. "Fuck me," he said, sweeping the glass onto a tray.

Later, he said that she was making a statement.

After my grandmother died, my parents paced the house. One time, they actually crossed paths in the family room.

Right away, they went at it. Whispered back and forth. Sonny and I sat on the couch watching TV. I switched it off. Sonny leapt onto the floor. Ran around and around my parents. In circles. The buttons on his pants clicking the hardwood.

They didn't look down. Just stared. Not at each other. At points on the wall behind their hair. I couldn't hear what they were saying. Just a few words — taxi, suitcase, and suicide — sputtered out.

Voices hissed and scratched. Eyes bulged. Heads shook. The longer they kept it up, the faster Sonny's hands and knees worked away on the hardwood. Finally, my father winced down. Looked back up at my mother. Sonny threw out a sharp bark. My father turned to me on the couch. "SHUT HIM THE FUCK UP."

My mother twisted slightly. My father caught her by the shirttail. She cried, tore away, ran up the stairs. My father stood there, staring at his empty hand.

Sonny still clicking. Around and around.

Once, a schoolboy licked a tin rooster. Walked all day with a rooster stuck to his tongue. Too scared and stupid to tell anyone. Boy's tongue got tired, yanked the rooster, and the tongue fell off.

Passed a bank machine. It's where people with money go. Thought maybe I'd get lucky. Lit a cigarette mashed on the floor. Slid against the wall, squatting and smoking.

In bustled a puffy parka. Legs curved like a horseshoe. She stood with her hands on her hips, shouting at me with her eyes.

"You can't be here," she croaked. She stood there, waiting for me to say something. "Can't you read?"

She pointed to a sign over my head. It said no smoking.

"This is a public area," she said.

"I know it's public," I said.

"It's one thing for you people to put your own health at risk, but it's another thing to risk other people's lives."

"I'm not risking lives," I cried.

"Are you making a transaction?"

I scrambled to my feet. "Yes."

"I don't see you making one. Where's your card?"

I stuck my hand in my pocket. Fished around.

"Where is it?" she said, a little louder now.

"You don't have to yell."

"Someone's got to take a stand. I'll call someone."

I'm not here. I'm never here. I'm on the bus. I'm everywhere. She took a step towards the phone.

"Fine," I said. I stubbed the cigarette out on this little tray they had in there. "Are you satisfied?"

She watched me do it. "No. I'm not satisfied."

"What do you want from me?"

I looked around at the ceiling, at the walls. There were cameras in there that took your picture.

"Yes," she said. "You can't hide."

"Don't you have anything better to do? I'm not surprised."

Her eyes narrowed. "What did you say? I want to know."

"No." Then I said very fast, "It's a free country."

She steadied herself against a cash machine. The whole thing was too much for her. I tensed up, ready for violence.

"You have no business being in here," she screamed.

"I'm freezing. Just a few more minutes, then I'll go."

She bent her head. I thought I might've gotten through. Then something snapped. She took quick, desperate steps towards the security phone like someone pulling a child from a car wreck.

"Fine. Go call someone. Fuck."

She picked up the phone. Opened her mouth to say something. I was already out the door screaming, "You're fat and evil!"

I didn't do it.

But I really really really wish I had.

Things happen to people: Nicky Posner, abortion. Marilyn Black, OD. Danny Clemente, parents divorced. Darlene Jaffe, parents dead in plane crash. Lisa Bellows, surgical dad cheating with surgical nurse.

When things happen to people, they radiate a light. Because they've got a picture caught inside them. Because they were there, and you weren't. And because you've only got a piece. And because all you can do is shrink and blow up that one tiny piece.

Until it explodes.

I walked until I heard a car come up over the hill behind me. I thought I saw my father's car standing there, exhaust foaming, windows steaming. Must've been a ghost. It was just a matter of time until somebody saw me and told somebody.

I escaped just in time. Slid along the shiny street.

There was nothing to do except ride. Around and around. I didn't know where. I don't care. I'm just killing time.

People get on, people get off. Nobody's like me — trying to reach the end. You think you find someone — like that man, laughing into his hands. Then he pulls the string to make the bus stop. It gets so you hate the sound of the doors opening or the sign that says *Stop Requested* because the feeling when the person starts looking for their stop is the worst feeling in the world.

Did you see that triangle of light? Must be Christmas. Lights swinging, music jingling. We never got Christmas.

"Why not?"

"Because we're Jews."

I know about history.

A pharoh watched us crush stone. He watched and laughed. A brick of hair grew out of his chin. Made us cross the desert. Eat flat bread tasting like paper stacked in a box.

"Why are we Jews?"

"Because we don't believe Christ was the son of God."

In our family, we don't believe in anything.

Myra Bernie's got a picture of him turning into Elvis. Sometimes it's Elvis, sometimes it's Christ. I like the way he looks on the cross. I like his long bleeding arms, his crying eyes.

At night the buses ran further apart. I spent a lot of time just walking around, freezing and swearing. Houses with families in them watched TV. Light oozed out windows. TV lights burst and jumped. Changed shape. Danced across a curtain.

I didn't know the time, only that it was night.

You can only stay on a bus so long.

I got off. Felt in the dark. From far away, a light bobbled. I ran across the street. It was the 7-Eleven. A man sponged the countertop, handed change to customers. Smiled. Said have a nice day. Had a pointy beard. Looked like Satan.

Satan's reflection stared at me from the refrigerated doors. Made me feel stupid. He was the one who should feel stupid with 7-Eleven all over his clothes. I opened a magazine. I've never read a whole magazine, not even an article. Just those little milestones. The lives of famous people who did something, the lives of famous people who died, the lives of famous people who did something awful — neat and pure and distilled into one hole. I admire how they do that, distil an entire life.

Tracey Berkowitz runs away. Tracey Berkowitz, female, fifteen, escapes from near death. Tracey Berkowitz, just fifteen, has two children and a dog and has just completed her first record album. Critics are raving about Tracey Berkowitz, just fifteen, who killed her parents in a bloody —

Billy Speed would laugh in their glossy faces if they put him in a magazine. He didn't need to be in one to make him a star.

Satan's eyes burned me around the store.

"I'm a customer," I said.

"If you buy something."

"OK," I said. "I don't want to spend my money here any more."

I ran out into the snow. I'm not just another runaway. I have a boyfriend. Not some convenience store loser.

And he opened his eyes and burned me to the ground.

I was lucky. Him. Me. Everything. Perfect. God. We did it. Everywhere. Under a stairwell. In a park. Against a tree. Under a salad bar. I traced the tracks on his arms and turned them into a charm and hung them around my neck where my heart beats.

Wrist by wrist, I pinned him down. Tore his pants from his legs. His back arched under me. I held his legs under me. His face sighed into me and his eyes closed and began to vibrate softly softly softly until his face became a little Jesus on the cross.

A world divided by horses.

Horses live in the country. They clomp through dirt and mud. In the country, wild horses gallop against dirt roads. Dust rises, blurring everything.

Horses live in the city. Their hoofs beat over concrete streets. In the city, trained horses clomp across stone. Twigs snap and splinter underneath their hoofed feet.

Feel my grandmother again. DNA clicking on timers. Nothing you can do to keep the good in and the bad out.

Love is dangerous. It's something to run away from. Baba wanted to swallow the sun. She ran all the way to the edge of the world but when she got too close the edge ran away.

Baba walked across Poland, escaping the men — the ones on horses and the uniformed ones who spoke in a hard foreign language and sprayed the streets with fire. She walked from shtetl to shtetl, finding them in flames or burnt up, bodies nailed to the jambs of doors, curling in the sun like strips of leather or salted tongue, until she made it to Minsk and then to Pangnirtung and then to Paris and finally to here where I'm from. Stone fences crumbling, broken barns shivering like the long ash of one of my mother's cigarettes. She hid, creeping out from the woods like she grew there, tangled and clotted with mud.

For nine months of their lives, my mother and my grand-mother each walked around with a tiny girl caught inside them. Not like a picture you shrink, blow up, and keep inside. This girl grew and shot out. Just like I grew inside and shot out of my mother, my mother shot out of my grandmother. Every-thing good dies fast. Everything rotten always lasts. Flowers shrivel as soon as they bloom. Weeds shoot up everywhere and eat the grass.

Sure, my grandmother's dead. But for the second it takes your eye to catch the wisp of a dandelion seed before it joins the sky, she knew love.

Forty-five years ago. Paris in springtime. A dirty girl coated with mud dazzled crowds on the rue Saint-Michel. Pine cones stuck in her hair, underwear hung in rags. The cold air still rose off the Seine and blushed Baba's skin like a bottle of pink champagne. There, in the city of love, Baba searched for light. Zaida was there for advanced studies in corporal mime. It was love at first bite. Zaida wasn't Zaida then. He was more than Zaida. He was ultra-Zaida. Teetering along the Seine. Right near the Cathedral du Notre Dame. His striped shirt rippled his chest. There was no easel. There was no canvas, but Zaida did what Zaida did best. He was painting the Cathedral du Notre Dame. Fingers streaking the air — thick, fast, hard. Steeples. Gargoyles. Baba stepped up. Scared. Shy. Vulnerable. A little girl in rags and tortured feet. She extended her moist hand. Stuck it straight into Zaida's pocket. What she felt was warm, thick, pulsing. She pulled her hand out. A white dove flew from Zaida's pocket and shot into the blue sky. Zaida covered his mouth with his hand. Like he was surprised. Like this. At the moment the bird hit the sky, Zaida turned into a horse. His mane was chestnut brown. Sleek. Shining. His mouth open, foaming. His teeth big, square, gleaming white. Baba pulled Zaida by the mane. Jumped on. They rode down under the bridge and swirling next to the rotting stinking Seine Baba grabbed Zaida's chestnut mane and pulling pulling pulling she began to do it. Riding Zaida. Each of her knees on Zaida's narrow pony hips. Paris was blurring the red bickering lips of intellectuals. Paris was blurring the red flickering ends of cigarettes. Paris was blurring the red sticking, staining Baba's thighs as they bounced bounced bounced over baguettes and botteilles du vin and bourgeoisie. Bouncing so fast, the wind whipped Baba's hair behind her. Bouncing so fast she couldn't catch her breath.

Sleeping in the leaves under the bridge, Zaida's legs wrapped around her hips, his dark hair rubbing against her back, she fell into her first sleep for weeks. Baba had a dream. She lifted, floating towards Zaida, golden fields spreading around them like honey. He asked her what she wanted. She fell and clung to him. Begged him to love her. He said, "I didn't promise you anything." She cried. He just yanked her hands from his legs and said, "No one died." Crawling and squirming awake, my grandmother rolled over to look at Zaida's beautiful face lying on the pillow of leaves beside her, but he was gone. She turned into the leaves, sniffing for what was left of Zaida, the dry leaves crumbling and burning her eyes back to sleep. Zaida, French, eyes the colour of the sky before it turns black, came back to say goodbye, leaning over my grandmother, blue eyes glinting, his kiss whipping her awake. On the horse. In the night. Dagger mouth. His heart beating him away forever.

After my grandmother died, my mother paced into a blur. Into a puddle. She slept, woke up, watched TV, smoked cigarettes, and picked her hands till the skin flicked up like pine cones and blood smeared on the walls and plates and she cried over and over why she'd been cursed with such rotten luck and how she'd married a bum and what made her kids such defective retards and how God hated her and how stupid stupid stupid she'd been and then she stopped.

"I can't do this any more," my mother shrieked from the kitchen. "It's on you, now. I hope you can handle it."

"If you're going to sing that tune, I'll leave you to it," he said. He stared at her. She stood there, looking down.

He paced. Pulled his mouth like a rubber toy. Tore his shirt till his chest hair popped. Light glistened the hair. Made it look wet. "What about family? Are you going to forget about us?"

She turned away. Back vibrating like the washing machine.

Next thing, I heard the door slam. Engine warmed up outside. Car crunched back and forth through the snow and pulled away.

One hour later, he came back.

Girls shivered in their underwear. Even with the blizzard coming men walked in and out of doors marked Pussy Cat and Cumming Attractions. Neon blinked. A cowboy lassoed the sky. A pig with a bag of money. An eagle scaled the sky, going nowhere.

People whisper when they talk to the bus driver late at night. Ladies with pails, heads wrapped like picnic baskets in flowered kerchiefs, and men clutching lunchbuckets with big gnarled fingers.

I rolled the hood of my parka and made a pillow. Hugged the edge of the bus between the seat and the window, motor panting. A man sat across the aisle, Hate and Kill tattooed on his forehead.

I must've drifted off.

The bus bumped and my head hit the glass and woke me up. Tattoo Man leaned against me.

"How old are you?" he asked me.

"Forty," I said.

"You don't look forty."

"Forty-five, actually."

"Cuppa sugar," Tattoo Man said.

"What do you mean?" I asked him.

He nodded to the bus seat. "You live here?"

"I guess so," I said.

"Makes us neighbours," he said, nodding back into his seat.

Something happened to the girl with no tits. SOMETHING ACTUALLY HAPPENED. A boy fell on the girl like a star. Made a hole.

Billy Speed stood there. Swagger mouth. Leaning against the lockers, smoke foaming between his fingers.

You can't smoke in school. He did. In one second, the girl's heart smashed to a million billion pieces. In one second, the girl with no tits wanted to swallow him to get that feeling over and over. It wanted to put Its mouth all over his mouth and go down down down until It disappeared. It wanted to burn up in the sky with him. It wanted to drown in water.

Billy Speed didn't have a group. He almost never went to class. He leaned against his car that was three colours of rust. He robbed purses. Couldn't help it. Came from Division, a poor area where people have barbecues and car parts rusting to death in the front yard.

His eyes slashed It to pieces.

Those eyes. The colour of the sky before it turns black. It wanted to crawl inside those eyes and sit there.

He never talked to the girl. If he ever did, It would faint. Die. Implode. Freeze into a cube. It didn't care. He made It want to sit in flowers. Not like Its mother's flowers. Wild flowers too perfect and beautiful the way the wind whipped through his hair. It held Its breath, not wanting to blow out this perfect perfect picture that shrank and expanded because the picture was caught inside the girl like a charm, like a little gold chain It once wore. And none of those other kids would ever see the picture — maybe they would only see a piece and would wonder and examine and discuss the tiny piece they'd found.

Soon, everyone knew. God. It was so obvious and grotesque. It sat. Steps of the school. Halls of the mall.

It wore different clothes. These jeans everyone wore with the star on the pocket. Those boots with the square heels It obviously bought and wore the exact same day because the leather was so new it was tragic and hideous. School stopped making sense. Everytime It put something in Its mind, the thing fell out.

It stopped answering questions.

Billy Speed never answered questions.

It stopped putting Its hand up.

He never put his hand up.

It stopped reading.

Everyday in school It pretended to read but It always looked around because maybe maybe maybe he'd turn around from his desk — hair, rustling, jungling like vines — and look at It.

Maybe if It counted to one hundred.

Ninety-nine.

He didn't look.

Ninety-nine-and-a-half.

Please, God, please make him look.

Ninety-nine-and-three-quarters.

Please please please. Oh, God I'll give up fifty years of my life if he just looks at me.

Okay, a hundred years.

It promised Itself It would only think about Billy Speed for one hour a day — after homework between eight and nine at night — until It had to remind Itself every second about that one hour and It just decided to think about Billy Speed every second until he became every second of Its life till Billy Speed became life.

It will wear those jeans — the ones with the star on the pocket — and those boots with the square heels.

He'll pinch a cigarette between his fingers. He'll take a drag, blow that drag between his lips. He'll look at the girl with eyes the colour of the sky before it turns black and he will see heaven, and the pictures of all those other girls floating inside his head will blow away like the clouds of the cigarette and he'll see only the girl inside himself and the world will stop.

Love will whirl through his mind like little tornadoes.

Underneath the moonlight, stars will shoot down on them. He'll wrap his leather jacket around Its shoulders and It will shiver and It will close Its eyes and Billy Speed will kiss It and he will plant those kisses on Its body like tiny flowers.

And people will see — they will actually see what the girl sees when It catches the edge of Its reflection blurring in the dirty windows of buses and convenience stores where It actually looks almost normal — and that kiss will last forever. The girl will put that kiss on Its dresser and It will hold its breath, staring at that kiss like a beautiful blue shard of glass It found somewhere.

Before the blizzard actually hit, only a little snow drifted outside like the medallions threaded through the fringe of my cowboy jacket. The driver skidded the bus along the ice and the people on the bus flew forward and back like bodies after a bullet spray. The driver grinned, watching the scene in his mirror.

People climbed off, threatening to complain to the city.

"I'm happy to be retiring tomorrow," said the driver.

A girl got on. I thought it was a girl, anyway, because she wore shorts and a little girl's parka and mewled from the street in her little girl's voice.

"Dri-ver," she called. "Dri-ver. Wa-it. Wa-it."

"Fuck," the driver said.

She was on all fours, climbing on.

"Thank you, driver," she said, rising and falling into him.

"Fuck," he said, pushing her back with his hands. "This has just got to take the cake."

"No. Really really really no." She fumbled around for change, pulling out a bill. "I don't have any change."

"Don't worry about it," he said.

She staggered to the back. Looked around. She wasn't a girl. The seats were empty except a crippled man with twisted stick legs who'd sat grinning at me since he climbed aboard. The woman plopped into the seat next to mine. Where her shorts hiked up, the skin bubbled like melted cheese.

She sat down and leaned me into a pole.

"I feel like crying," she said.

Right then and there, her head fell forward. She showed me a five dollar bill crumpled in her stumpy little hand. I took the bag of change from my pocket and held it in front of her bobbling head.

The crippled man gleamed from the long seat across the way. "Come here. I'll help you with that."

Her head jerked back like a chicken.

The bus pulled to a stop. She got up, swinging around the chrome pole, holding out her bill in one hand and my bag of money in the other. "I've almost got the change, Driver," she yelled.

"I don't care," the driver sang.

A big broad man got on. Something glinted from his jacket.

"Our boys in blue," the driver said.

The cop moved to the back.

I wanted to ask the policeman. To move my body. To ask. Then something happened I don't completely understand. The crippled man and the woman climbed all over each other. They moaned and yelped. Hands twisted around necks. Fingers scratched. Mouths bit.

The cop rushed over and pulled the woman off. He dragged her over to the exit doors, banging on the doors until the driver pulled to a stop. The doors squeaked open. The cop threw the woman into the snow. I looked out the window. She spread out in the snowbank like a bag of garbage.

I ran off the bus and watched it sail away. Down in the snow, I knelt at her side. "Where's my money?" I asked.

"I just got mugged by a cop and a cripple," she said.

She fell back into the snowbank, squeezing it like a pillow, a million flakes of snow exploding in the sky.

I'd hate to be snow. Even if it's true that every flake's different, they're still the same to me. Stars are better. They hang in the sky. People stretch their eyes looking for them. They shed sparks. Have names. You can't touch them. They don't melt.

Pregnancy was the cause.

Made them buy the house. The car.

"You were the result of that," my father explained one fucked-up night I won't forget because he drank an entire bottle of Jack Daniels. Waved the bottle. Teetered on the edge of my bed.

Because they didn't love each other.

"It wasn't love," he said. "Maybe once. Not now. It's natural. It's the way these situations go."

But they made a decision.

"We'll stay together. For the sake of the children."

"Don't bother," I told him.

"Really?" His eyes brightened. He reviewed his new life. Without her. Without us. That new boat he always wanted. That fishing cabin. Guilt got him and the hope vanished. "Also, there's the issue of alimony and child support," he said.

"You've got to consider all the angles," I said.

Men buy girls' panties. Myra Bernie told me. Girls in school like me. Unpopular girls. Girls with big tits. Girls with regular tits. Girls with no tits at all. The men don't even care. Panties come out of a machine like a chocolate bar. The men take them home and cuddle them like a cat. She told me. Myra Bernie. Because her parents heard it at a party. I don't care. I don't even like panties. The word sickens me.

I was broke. I knew what this meant. I'm not stupid.

I wasn't going to social services. I don't know where that is. I guess they have an office you call to get picked up. I guess someone comes by in a car and drives you around until they find a family willing to take you. I wasn't going with any family.

I went into a coffee shop and slumped in a booth.

A strung-out boy with bruised arms stared blankly from behind the counter. "Twenty bucks," he said like he was talking in his sleep. "Twenty bucks," over and over.

I didn't know what he meant. I didn't know if he was talking to me. I looked behind me. Nobody was there.

"That's a deal," he said. "That's a fucking good deal. It's not going to get any fucking better than that, believe me."

I told the boy I don't have any money.

"I know what you mean," he said, sadly.

Pulled back the foil lids of creamers. Watched myself twist upsidedown in tarnished spoons and picked the skin on my hands until they bloomed like wounds. The wounds of Jesus. Elvis. Someone.

Lit napkins on fire until the boy charged over. "Cut it out."

I stared up at the boy.

He didn't notice me, just poured into my cup.

"Christ," my father told me. "The shit's really hit the fan."

The more my mother melted into a puddle, the more he tip-toed into my room. I heard him outside. Back and forth. Slippers clapping the floor. Eventually, he came in. Sat on my bed. Sighed. Sometimes he cried, other times, he just sat there in the dark. Talked and talked. Like a bad TV show he forced me to watch. I glared at him. I didn't want to hear about his problems. Him. Her. He threw my grandmother in there, too.

"Fucking bitch. If it weren't for that fucking bitch."

"What?"

"Boat. Sunshine. Cabin. Your mother. Different. I don't know."

He'd unwind like that for hours. Once he got going, there was no stopping him. I didn't want to hear it. BECAUSE I HAD A MILLION PROBLEMS MYSELF, or whatever. And because I'm the most selfish person in the world.

"This will mean divorce," he said in the voice of a general.

"I know." I always agreed with whatever came out.

"You'll have to testify. Are you up to it?"

"You bet," I said.

At the end, he always said, "Don't tell your mother we had this conversation. If you do, I'll deny it."

This one last time. I heard him. Pretended I was asleep. Tugged the blanket over me. Shrugged down deep into my bed.

He stood there, at the foot of my bed. Minutes clicked by. Finally, I couldn't take it any more.

"I was asleep," I said.

"Oh," he said.

"Do we have to do this?" I said, making my voice tiny and sharp. "You woke me up."

"I'm sorry," he said. "I needed someone to talk to."

I heard him, ruffling in the dark like a bird, waiting for me to sit up. Say it was okay. Nobody said anything. Finally he left.

Curls smoked up from industrial towers. Birds hurtled from the sky like Japanese airplanes. Men loaded trucks with big sacks. Men packed meat, swinging bloody cows from hooks. Men. Men everywhere. Loading and unloading, breath steaming out their mouths and noses, eyes wincing, big teeth gritting and grinding against the cold.

I walked around, my mittens covering my stinging cheeks. I watched for Sonny. Thought I saw him — blurring off the edges, just a piece of ladies' underwear stuck in a snowbank.

Sonny and me walked around them careful like a fire. Afraid they'd catch and burn down the house.

"For a dog, you are very smart," I told Sonny.

The mall was shut up for the night. No cars in the lot. No people inside. No music squeezed out when I opened the doors. I walked through anyway, my skin burned as the cold came out. Grabbed food off the tables. Smoked a butt someone had thrown away. Sat on a plastic table. Heard a noise and slipped into the little garden filled with cigarette butts, wax cups, and shopping coupons. Plastic fronds bent around me like praying hands.

I hate the mall. Everybody goes there. Those kids. Same ones like in the park. Mangling like a thing with ten arms and legs, so you can't separate them out. Believe they've got a right. Like their parents own the fucking mall. Pretend they don't notice people staring. Wear black. Look serious and suicidal, eyes burning with secrets they think nobody else can understand.

Lying in the plastic garden, I couldn't help thinking this must be what happens to birds when they die. They hide so that nobody can find them, turning into bird dust. You never see a dead bird unless it bashes into a building or gets hit by a car. They're probably just more intelligent than humans. Don't want their parents hanging around, bugging the hell out of them.

One day under the naked elm. A bird kicked out. Just hatched. No feathers. Tiny pointed beak, legs, eyes — all shivering in jelly. Sonny and I stared. And stared. Poked it with a stick. Sonny asked me was it an accident? I told him, Of course, it didn't commit suicide. He wanted to know why don't you see birds just die? Use your brains, I told him. Why would a bird just die? From old age, he said. He went on like that. There was no stopping him.

Dust fogged around me. A garden gnome parted the plastic fronds, paused, and screamed, "Sweet loving Jesus." I rushed through the mall, my feet hardly feathering the floor.

I flattened my body against the floor of the department store at the end of the mall, sliding under the security door on my back. I ran to the back of the store. A fat security guard flashed a light in my eyes. I ran into the snow.

Once, a man was driving down the street. The car slipped on black ice, spun, flipped the car into a crackling bush. It was considered a mysterious disappearance until spring came and the snow melted out the car with the man inside, one block from his house.

I walked past a movie theatre with Coming Soon: Johnny "The Wad" Holmes Film Festival. Naked ladies stuck to windows.

Men stood in a line, handcuffed in the snow like a bracelet someone lost. Cops stood around like sides of beef.

The sky filled with snow.

I needed to pee.

It's hard to pee in the snow when it's forty below. I squatted. Looked around. Made sure nobody saw. Couldn't feel my legs. The pee started. Dribbled down my legs. I couldn't stop. It dribbled and ran. I tried to hold my legs apart. They cramped and shook together. The hot pee splashed on my pants, steaming.

I squiggled against the back of another bus. Right away, I knew it was all wrong. There were too many people for so late at night. Arms and legs stuck out like amputees. The only seat left was across from the driver. She called at me to put my feet on the floor. Looked at me over and over from the corner of her eye.

"You smell," she said like I murdered someone. "This isn't the Salvation Army."

Somebody cracked out a laugh.

I looked around at the passengers. They shrugged in their seats. Rolled their eyes. "What's so fucking funny?" I asked a skinny pursed-lipped troll.

"That's it," said the driver, pulling over.

"This isn't even a stop," I cried. I stood up. "It's not a stop," I said again a little louder.

"I don't want any trouble," she said.

"I'll call social services. You'll be sorry. It'll be in all the papers." I ran down the street, kicking the side of the bus.

I could find Sonny here. Even here in this darkness.

Sonny could be anywhere.

Nobody could know. He disappeared, again and again, shivering naked off the porch into the snow like a pirate off a plank. I pulled him out of the snow, legs tangling like kite tails between my bare hands, and carried him back inside a sunken ship.

Something muffled up in the snow behind me. I turned around. A creep slouched against a building. Snapped his teeth.

"Warm enough?"

"I'm okay."

Cold stabbed the tips of my fingers. My toes. It was all I could think about. I jumped around to make the pain go away.

"There's a blizzard," he said. LIKE I DIDN'T KNOW.

"I'm fine."

"Want a ride?"

"No. I don't know." I said very fast, "I've got a boyfriend."

"I don't see anyone."

Wind blew me around. Snow filled the sky so you couldn't see.

"If you're not happy, you can split."

"Really?"

Steam came out of my mouth and out of the creep's. He laughed like there was nothing to worry about.

"Sure." He held up his hand. "Put your life here." Huddled over and smiled up at me in a way that made me believe him.

"Okay."

I bit my hair.

He lit a cigarette.

"So where's your car?" I asked him.

"No car."

"I thought we were going for a ride."

"On the bus."

One rumbled past. He pitched his cigarette. Took my arm like it was expensive. We climbed aboard. I followed him through the door of the bus. The wind trumpeted. He was thin. Old. Older than my father. Wore a tight jacket, some kind of shiny vinyl or plastic, with a zipper. I followed him and we sat in the back of the bus. The bus driver yelled for the creep.

"Hey you," called the driver.

Silence from the bus.

"Last to come on," the driver yelled. "How do you expect to ride the bus without a ticket?" The creep took one of my hands and gently kissed it. "What's your name?" he asked me.

I couldn't remember.

All I could think was what would the girl with no tits think? What would Its mother think? Probably only losers talk to creeps. I talk to creeps all the time now. It's what I do.

The driver called, "Hey, what about it?"

Everyone yelled, "Shut the fucking doors."

Sickened me, everybody thinking maybe he was my boyfriend. He wasn't my boyfriend. I checked to see if anyone looked at us. Nobody did. They just yelled to shut the fucking doors.

The driver started the bus again. After a few stops, the creep pulled the string and made the bell ring. He led me down the stairs of the bus, down the street to the Mall Hotel and Bus Depot where intercity buses like this one come in and out. He clanked along the street like a person with one short leg.

"Metal plates," he said, nodding down. "I was lucky. They came like that."

Angry bus-riding cowboys filled the Mall Hotel bar. As we walked to a table, someone called the creep Lance. Lance touched the hands and shoulders of a few people along the way. They looked at me and smiled at Lance. I felt like the open petals of a cyclamen. One old lady teetered on the lap of a man with a leather vest and a hanger for a nose. She looked at me and laughed so hard, black stripes ran down her face.

We took a seat near the stage and waited for someone to bring our drinks. The zipper on Lance's jacket was pulled down. I saw his white hairless body. His dry papery lips. He ran his tongue over and over his teeth. "You're bleeding," he said. He shook his finger near his mouth. I touched my face. Blood came from my nose and mouth. I asked where the bathroom was. "Don't," he said, nodding. "I like it." He touched the tips of my fingers.

Glasses chinked along tables set up in thin rows. On the stage, a very old lady rolled around and around on a tiny blanket and stuffed animals that looked ratty and torn up and flattened just like the lady. She was naked. When she moved, the skin on her legs and stomach stretched out and hung like plastic bags.

People whooped and clapped. Lance banged his glass on the table. The waiter came by with a tray. Lance said he didn't want nothing, he was just making a point. The waiter lumbered away like a big dog who didn't give a shit. The head on the next table turned and veiny eyes rolled towards me. The head, a hockey puck with a ponytail, was attached to a body slumped over the table.

"Hey, hey," said the mouth belonging to the head.

Lance picked his lip, peeled off a medallion of skin, looked at it, and flicked it away. "Whatcha looking at?" he asked the man.

The man offered to stand on his head if I came over to his table. "Because you're so beautiful," the man said.

Lance looked over at me.

I shook my head.

"You'd better be joking," Lance told the man.

The man lifted his face. Pushed himself away from the table. Raised a knee, positioning himself. He knelt on the table and flattened his palms.

Everyone in the bar clapped.

Other men stood on their heads. A few fell onto the floor and swore out loud.

"Hey, fuck you," Lance said.

"Hey, fuck you. I'm just having a little fun," the man said.

"I don't give a fuck," Lance said. "I'm going to break your fucking mouth so it's lying over there on the floor."

Lance got up and wobbled. He inhaled and exhaled.

The men stared at each other.

The man laughed. Lance pulled back his arm.

They went at it. Bashed each other. Clutched and pounded and bit. Twirled around me. Every time one of the men got hit, something wet flew off him.

Nobody broke it up. Nobody cared. Even the waiter just roamed around with his tray, plunking glasses of beer on all the tables.

Lance stomped on the face of the other man. A pop like someone stepping on a balloon. Air gushed out. Lance got up. Staggered across the floor. Crashed a bottle and stuck glass into the head of another man. Fists cracked against bones.

The bar swirled, blood splurting from different parts of the men like cartoon barrels shot with bullets.

A man with a heavy moustache carried a tray of beer over to our table. He asked me what I wanted. I told him a Cinzano. I saw a lady in a magazine order it once. He said they only have beer. How many? I told him one beer. He glared at me and put a glass of beer on my table. He paused, then asked for his money. I pointed at Lance and said, "He's paying." The man picked up the glass of beer and moved to the next table. He didn't even wipe my table with a cloth the way they did at the Pony Corral.

Suddenly, I felt like I was going to throw up. I didn't want to throw up in there. I slid past the fighting. Ran up the stairs and down the street. Ran as fast as I could.

I remembered something from back when I was little. Sonny was barely born. My mother took Sonny and me for walks. My mother and I walked. She talked and talked. Words blowing over hills like tiny flowers. Pulled Sonny behind us in a little wagon. Led us down to an island near the river. We ate tuna-fish sandwiches. Not Sonny. He was too small. We fed him from a bottle. The wind and my mother's red hair blowing. Sonny in her arms wriggling, sandpaper voice rubbing away. Everything soft and blurry. And a story she told about a tiger. It must've been from India because that's where tigers come from. I can barely believe this happened. Must've been a dream of something else.

In India there was an adolescent tiger called Bob. Bob lived among the olive trees and Persian elms. Life was simple for him. One day, as he bent his head to nibble some grass and dandelions, something caught his eye. Vibrant orange and striped black. Bob needed to capture this creature, but whenever he turned to grab it, the thing moved out of his sight. Bob got so obsessed with having this thing that he chased it ferociously. The villagers watched Bob chase his own tail. The tail bones soft, not yet fully formed, whipped out from Bob's control, but Bob didn't know this thing he chased was his tail. He didn't believe it because it was beautiful and magnificent and he couldn't believe it belonged to him. Bob continued to chase his tail, intensely and unmercifully, till he whipped himself into a hot and stinking pool of butter.

Sonny just listened. And watched. The way he always did. He sucked. Milk drooled in his smirk. Just like my baby, squirming in my arms, wriggling away, that little smile already twisting.

I sat in the snow. It seeped through the cloth of my jeans. My eyes swelled. Tears dribbled down my cheeks, caught in my mouth. I ran up to this telephone booth and I thought I was going to call my mother and I was going to tell her the truth, how scared I was, how I needed to talk to her about things, how I needed her to tell me what I should fucking do because I was so confused and scared, and I ran and ran and when I got up to the phone booth I just started kicking and yelling at the booth FUCK ME FUCK ME FUCK ME until I got tired and fell down and all these pieces of glass flickered with the moon.

This girl. Darlene Strombelli. Handed out candy in the school-yard. A fat girl nobody played with who talked slow from the sides of her mouth. Everybody talked about Strombelli.

My father watched my mother on the couch. She sat there. Screwed up tight. Mouth a cramp. Eyes like big naked windows, watching herself in the TV. It wasn't on. She didn't say anything. He didn't say anything.

From the kitchen, the refrigerator was humming.

He looked afraid. She liked it. Whenever she moved, she jerked him towards her by a string. Ordered him around with her eyes. If he died, nobody would look after her. She'd crumple away.

He pursed his lips. Shrilled like a woodpecker. Glanced over. She stared at him like he'd farted out loud. He winced away.

We sat there. My mother, father, and me.

The air crackled.

Out of nowhere, his lips curled to a twitch. He said, "Don't be a Strombelli."

That meant don't give candy away.

"No kid of mine should be seen buying her friends."

AS IF I WOULD.

I'D NEVER DO IT IN A MILLION BILLION YEARS.

We didn't have candy anyway.

WE DIDN'T EVEN HAVE CANDY.

His eyes gleamed around the house. Threw his voice like a taunt, "Don't be a Strombelli."

He smirked. Narrowed his eyes at me like he knew something about me. I wanted to run from the family room. Down the hall. Through the door. Hide inside the snow.

"I'd never do it," I said in a tiny little voice.

"Don't be a Strombelli," my father sang again.

"I'D NEVER DO IT," I screamed.

"Well, it's something your grandmother would do," he said. Then he smiled at my mother. "Only it wasn't candy she gave away."

"Do you think I'm like her?"

I looked at him. At her.

"I don't know." His eyes glinted at my mother. She began to giggle, squirling in her couch. "It's too early to tell."

I ran away to my room. Slammed the door. Cried into a corner.

I had dreams about chopping their heads off. Burning them in their beds. Flames crackling, screams tearing down the walls and up into the sky like magic scarves vanishing into birds.

Sonny panted up to my hand while my father kept it up downstairs. I heard them through the floorboards.

"Stop it," my mother shrieked. "I'm going to pee my pants." She liked when he was mean. It was the only time she liked him.

I stumbled in the snow. I was still a little afraid. I walked around the building. Around and around the building, just to calm down a little bit, until I realized it wasn't a building. It was what was left of the telephone booth.

The snow kept falling.

The stars pulled me closer to Sonny. And the moon. They pulled the water back and forth like a bedsheet.

A little city hospital sat beyond hedges on the edge of a busy street. Just outside, an ambulance screamed its head off and ran away. I was crying all over the place. I couldn't stop. I'd fucked myself up. I knew that. I knew it was the stupidest week of my life. Around the lobby inside, a man in white wheeled a screaming girl, toes pointed like a dancer or a stroke victim. He whispered, "It's going to be okay now, take it easy." A man with glass in his head shouted at a nurse, "I AM AN EMERGENCY." People wandered around in paper gowns. They shuffled around in paper slippers. People looked like they belonged somewhere. A smell of antiseptic and TV dinners hung in the air. I wanted to glide through those Emergency doors.

There's this man, I read in a magazine, who fucked this girl while he strangled her to death. He put life into her while life came out of her. That's what he said. Life goes in, life goes out.

A couple of security guards laughed and drank coffee. People walked around, missing a shoe, covered in bloody sores. Every person in that lobby had at least one open sore. I stood in the hall when the nurse came by. She pushed a metal thing with files.

I wanted to ask. To find out. To know. "I want —"

Her eyes screwed together. Made her face pinch. Waited for me to say something. I had something to say. I really did.

"What?" she asked. She looked mad, then she forced a smile.

I didn't know how to ask. My stupid mouth opened, but all

I could say was, "I need to be locked up. For everybody's protection. What do you need to do to get a room around here?"

"You should go to the information desk."

She pointed where a lady sat. In the waiting area, a big TV hung chained to a wall. People stared at a late-night movie.

"WHAT?" I screamed. "SIGN SOMETHING?" I imagined them calling my parents. I didn't want to see them. "Will they tell my parents?"

"If you're under eighteen."

I wanted to ask her, but the words clogged in my throat.

"What's wrong with you?" she said.

"They can't know," I sobbed.

"Tell me," she said. "Is it mental or physical?"

I thought about it. "Mental."

"You're in the wrong place." She pointed back out the door. "That hospital is across town."

It wasn't until later that I realized you could be both.

Sonny can't be outside. HE CAN'T. You don't know. He couldn't survive. Sharp wet blades of grass. Beating of lawn-mower blades. Air conditioner blades making everything cold like supermarkets. Elm trees stripped half-naked. Naked. Even in the summer, branches spearing. "They're dying," my mother said. "Nobody can save them. Even the city."

"He must be trained," my father said.

There was nothing anyone could do. Sonny escaped. Over and over. Even after my mother locked all the doors and windows, we still saw him from the living-room window, racing behind the truck that sprayed the mosquitoes, appearing and disappearing in the fog.

"God. God. God," my mother screamed. "It's poison."

"Shut up," said my father. "We'll get him checked by the doctor."

"His babies will be deformed," she said.

"So they'll be deformed," he said.

Sonny knew about the poison. The papers screamed it. He didn't care. JUST WANTED TO SEE WHAT WOULD HAPPEN.

Or, this other time we ate the cherries.

"Over the plate. Over the plate," my father showed us, sticking out his chin. Sonny didn't care about stains. He stuffed the cherries in his cheeks. Raced through the door, down the street. Cherry flesh jewelling and staining. Sonny, sitting on a curb, smirking out the bones.

Okay, so so so one day the girl with no tits had razorburn. Why? Because Its parents bought It a hair removal system after many visits to the dermatologist. Why? Because It had little hairs on Its arms, legs, face — LIKE EVERYONE — and because Its parents stared into the girl's face, turning it back and forth under the light, pointing at strands creeping out from the girl in places where hair was never seen in glossy magazine photographs.

"What should we do?" Daddy looked at Mommy.

"Why are you asking me?" said Mommy, voice leaping like a circus pony. "Am I hirsute?"

"No," said Daddy quickly, creeping under his words. "But you're a woman, aren't you?"

"Lend her your razor," said Mommy.

Daddy bent his head. "Oh, I'm going to be sick."

The hair removal system can only be used once every three weeks. The girl's hair grew faster. Tiny black thorns sprung out.

Miss Dorchester was the circus freak hired by the school to teach socials. Because Miss Dorchester had no arms or legs, the principal, Mrs. Sakamoto, wheeled her into the class.

David Goldberg — that skinny hairless little prick — had just taped the answers to the test onto the front of Dorchester's desk where everybody could see them but her, but not before he jumped to the front of the class and said, "Does anyone know what the girl's tits look like?" He chalked two dots on the board, cracking the class into squealing-pig laughter.

Tits were crucial. At our school the girls wore their tits like medals. They walked with their chests out. They walked like this. All over our school, big fat tits floating separate from the girls who wore them.

Debbie Dodge — who everyone loved and who had big tits

that she lifted and thrusted and thrusted in boys' faces and who didn't deserve to clean Billy Speed's runners with her mouth — she honked into her hands like a sick mallard. The girl with no tits pretended It didn't know what everyone was laughing at, squirming in Its seat, hoping, praying everything died down before Billy Speed came to class.

Billy Speed was always late.

He didn't write tests.

They wheeled Dorchester in. Everyone began the test. Tittering. Crumpling. The girl, who was never in on anything, saw a note drift around and around the room. Dorchester was oblivious, perched behind her desk, head rotating back and forth like an owl. The girl Itself was trying to pay attention pay attention pay attention when the note came to Its desk. The girl read the note calmly like It had nothing to do with the note even though the note said THE GIRL WITH NO TITS HAS RAZORBURN.

Dorchester asked what was going on.

The girl said nothing. Just sat there, staring at the note.

"What is that?" Dorchester said, leaning, careful, careful not to tip over. "What is that piece of paper? Bring it to me."

The girl held the note and felt the flames of power crackling around It, and everybody waited to see what It did — or didn't do — and and and all the kids vibrated with scary excitement and Dorchester said bring it up. The girl said no.

"Bring it up," Dorchester screamed.

The girl jumped up and screamed no again.

Dorchester said, "It will go to the principal."

The girl looked around at faces blurring, voices raking the inside of Its head. It wanted to burn the faces with fire. It wanted to drown the voices with water. It screamed "SHUT THE FUCK UP" — something It never ever did because It was such a vomitty little suck — and the whole class went silent.

It squeezed Its eyes to make the whole scene go away. The whole time It kept looking over at the door, screaming inside O Billy, Billy don't see, don't come in now, and It prayed and It hoped to God Billy O Billy didn't come in and that the door didn't bang open for him to see It like this. O Billy Billy Billy — don't let him walk in now, don't let the door bang open, don't let him decide to actually show up on time for once. It stood in the middle praying, burning, don't let him find out I'm the It girl, please God.

The girl got up from behind Its desk. It walked over to Dorchester with the note.

Everyone waited, scared, breath held. Dorchester didn't even read the note. "Throw it out," she ordered It, skinny tongue clucking out, little head working back and forth.

Everyone burst into laughter. Dorchester barked for everyone to get back to the test. The kids chanted, "razorburn, razorburn, razorburn." The girl with no tits shook and said, "Rayburn," pretending It didn't know what they were saying, trying to confuse them. "I DON'T LOVE STEVE RAYBURN," It howled. But everyone knew It was bluffing and one kid — that bitch Debbie Dodge with the big tits who started the whole thing — even looked at the girl like It was dumb and corrected It, "*Razor*burn, not Rayburn."

It knew It was fucked. It jumped up and eeked like a mouse. Everyone enjoyed that immensely. They screeched the girl through the halls of the school and through the schoolyard, following It like the tail of a kite. It finally broke away from the tail and took a shortcut.

The sun slashed It to pieces. It stumbled and gangled. Tears dribbled from Its eyes — the trees, cars, buildings smearing.

It ran in a straight line all the way home through Blue Jay Park. Where It ABSOLUTELY WASN'T ALLOWED because It would get murdered. IT WOULD GET KILLED. Only certain kids are even allowed there who all know each other and whose parents belong to the tennis club that's very expensive. Your parents must make a lot of money. Drive a European car. Blue Jay Park where they once stuffed a hard horse turd in Its mouth and held It down until It almost choked. Blue Jay Park where they once lifted Its stiff body and stuffed It into a shopping cart, rattling the cart through the parkade across the pavement, over speed bump and speed bump, until the cart tipped. Blue Jay Park where they tortured It behind a thorny bush. Held It down. Their eyes narrowed like the eyes of wolverines. They licked their lips. Smiled sharply. Watched It squeal and squirm. Stuck it with sticks. Whacked It with their arms. Arms a rotating blur. Up and down like Ferris-wheel chairs.

The girl ran through the park. Certain kids tangled up, making out. They didn't notice the titless girl while It ran past them all the way home. It didn't say anything to Its parents. In the past they'd looked away with rage and disgust because WHAT DID THE GIRL EXPECT ANYWAY? It never listened to the Dale Carnegie tapes they bought, never practised the dance steps they taught, never went to school dances like all the other little girls. Mommy and Daddy tried. Slapped Its hands from Its face. Took It to Alphonse at Hair Magic where everyone went. Sent It to lessons. Leaned suggestions against Its cereal bowl. Poked, adjusted, and tried to fix It. They couldn't accept that It was defective. And so the girl with no tits locked Itself inside Its stupid room and hoping and praying so hard It snapped in half, so there were two girls walking around.

I circled the block two or three times before I went to the bus shelter. Kids at school say a man lived there. It smelled like B.O. People had carved their initials in the wood. Two girls curled together, makeup smeared across their open mouths.

I went into Chunky Chicken to use the bathroom. I stuck my hands under the faucet. Made the sink black. No paper towels. Just toilet paper. Couldn't get all the dirt off. The paper tore and dissolved between my fingers. Pieces stuck to the counters and the floor. A lady came in with her kid. Took one look. Ordered the kid out. The kid screamed. "You'll go at home," she hissed back.

It was early morning, but people were still walking around in paper chicken heads. Dumb fat girls ate chips, staring out of blank eyes. I sat in the plastic booth. A man in a chicken uniform came around to clear the tables.

"You're not a customer of Chunky Chicken," he said.

"I'm eating here, aren't I?" I said.

"You didn't pay for that food."

"It's in my mouth," I said. "I'm chewing it."

"Did you or did you not pay money for that food?" he said. He made me take the chicken out of my mouth and drop it on his tray.

The sun dulled like a penny behind layers of snow. All over the street, cars broke down like dead Indian cows. Strangers huddled in bus shelters. Faces clenched and unclenched behind windshields. People waved their arms for the bus to stop. A man fell to his knees in the snow behind one bus.

Once, in the early morning, a newspaper delivery girl forgot to wear her parka with the reflectors on. A snowblower roared by, mixed the girl in the snow like hamburger meat.

Maybe I'll stick my tongue on a lamppost. That's how they'll find me. Maybe I'll reach out with my lips and kiss his eyelids. Now look what you've made me do. It didn't matter if I saw anybody. I don't care about friends or dancing at those stupid school dances where everybody just stands around anyway except a few jocks and student council geeks. I'd rather die than be seen at one of those. I fingered his ribs and the little muscles in his stomach.

He took orders. Whatever I'd say. Snapped my fingers in the air above his head. Jumping up and falling back down.

Even in that snow I couldn't stop my eyes fidgeting for something shiny and bright — a pretty boy, parties, lights. Whenever a scraggly doll looked in my direction, I gave him the eye. I smiled at the boys in coffee shops and malls until their doors locked. I twitched from a million cups of coffee I never paid for and watched the boys flick by. Tuques pushed back on their gorgeous heads. Student boys sticking their faces in books. Business boys strutting out in Armani suits. Artist boys smelling like paint thinner. Biker boys swaggering in leather pants. Pony boys knocking their long skinny legs together. Skate boys flicking in and out of the streets like fireflies. Even not so gorgeous boys. I'd marry him. If he'd ask me. I'd do it in a minute. In a second.

With each step, he steps into my heart.

He floats.

Inside me.

I fall apart, splitting into skinny glass splinters.

Beauty tortures. How come beauty burns everything away so the rest of the world — even me — disappears?

Some of the boys glanced up. I smiled, hoping to crack the distance between them and me. They didn't smile back. They flicked cigarettes into metal ashtrays. One sauntered by, eyes flashing up at me. I didn't care. Only losers notice me. In the next booth, some boys and one girl sat. A boy lifted his hand. His fingers flicked one of the girl's tits. The boys just watched. Didn't speak. Didn't smile. Didn't move. Were serious and religious.

After, the girl slumped in the corner. I would've been happy. I would've rolled the whole thing over and over between my fingers.

The boys talked and roared. "Well, that's a given," one said. They went on eyeing the crowd, joking and punching each other. A limp pale man — a Kleenex — asked if I wanted anything. I sat in the plastic booth. The Kleenex reached into his apron and pulled something out. I ran into the snow.

Myra Bernie once told me if you swallow a boy's cum you got a piece of the boy inside you. If you swallow a piece of a smart boy, then you got smarter. If the boy was dumb, nothing changed.

I want Billy Speed to put his cock inside me and say I love you in that order. Then I won't be afraid to die.

Birds and bugs and bees die after they fuck.

I kept seeing Sonny as I rode on the bus. His eyes. Everywhere. I'll hold him. We'll warm each other up. Me and Billy Speed and Sonny will become a family. A happy famous heroin-addicted family. If you're famous it doesn't even matter if you're dead because you're still beautiful. Look in the magazines. It's in there.

There was this boy on another bus. He was a babe, a fucking gorgeous babe. Not a zit. Just some gorgeous boy sitting with some ordinary girl. The whole scene bugged me. BUGGED ME. You had to wonder what he was doing with her. Thighs you want to lick over. And over. Arms pumping with big ropy veins — guitar veins, smack veins — I couldn't really see because he wore a coat. I could only imagine. I could fuck anyone with veins like that. I could fuck a girl. I could even fuck a girl with veins like that.

I was sick of being alone. I'm human. I've got needs. I stared at the boy. Even with the girl there. I didn't care. I had nothing to lose. Nobody treats Tracey Berkowitz like shit. Boys get humongous boners when they see me. They all want to fuck me. Thin wet doors vibrate open and closed, knives rush in.

The boy winced away. Stared at his own lap. The girl caught my eye and laughed. I saw her laugh WITH THAT LITTLE WET MOUTH.

"FUCK YOU, CUNT," I yelled. "Yeah, you. I'm not kidding." They both stared down, smirking, LIKE THERE WAS SOMETHING WRONG WITH ME. "YOU BET THERE IS, CUNT," I yelled. "I just escaped from the nutbarn for killing a cunt like you."

I'm not what you think. I'm not junk. I'm not a dink. I'm not garbage flowers you leave to rot and stink and smell and curl up all dry and papery so they crumble as crusty as the flowers on this fucked up shower curtain. I'm not like that, I'm —

Drops of ice on the window made it look like I was crying. I was crying anyway. Icicles pointing off a burnt building. Me. Just a raggedy black hole firemen spray with a hose.

There's no such thing as true love. I want to kill God.

The moon fell behind a building. I got off the bus and ran through the black. Snow humps rising around me like whales.

Cars made a rubber smell. I covered my nose. Felt something wet. Blood dribbling down my face. People on the street looked at me LIKE IT WAS A BIG DEAL, like it was their noses.

Somebody must've found Sonny, right? That's what happens when things get lost, right? You can't be lost forever, can you?

Sonny disappearing is like me disappearing.

People looked at me, then looked away, like I'm an accident. I am, only I was born this way. Sonny and me. We were both born accidents. FUCKING BASTARDS.

All these thoughts were rushing through my head.

FUCKING ASSHOLES.

PIECESASHIT.

I realized my mouth had been moving. Sounds were coming out. I wanted to take off my clothes and burn a hole through the ice. This dog I saw limping through the streets, its barking, pointed face. The snow, the dog, disappearing.

EVERYTHING'S ALREADY HAPPENED. But Sonny will be okay. He really will, you know, because he's planted inside my brain like a seed and he'll come out somehow in an idea or a dream. Did you know the weakest gene survives? Look at me. I'm here, aren't I?

My feet were crying. The problem, the problem, the problem was I lost all my feelings. This is the first sign of gangrene. Almost everyone in my family has got gangrene. It's in our chromosomes. One day we're fine, then the next day, gangrene. First your fingers, then your arms, legs, and before you know it, they've got you in a little basket and they're carrying you around the mall.

I stumbled onto a bus. My head kept banging on the window. A lady looked over. Face screwed into a pig's tail. She perched on the seat by one ass cheek. Probably she never took the bus. But there she was. And she had to sit down to read her dumb magazine — *Golf Widows*, or whatever. Then I felt something hot bubble out. The lady lowered her magazine, let it sink in, then screeched through the crowd.

I wanted to laugh and cry.

My name is Tracey Palomino. Fifteen. I'm riding the seven seas. But I'll find my brother. I'm not getting off this bus until I do.

I'll find you Sonny.

Snapping at my heels. Head thrown back. Mouth a howling circle. Dragging along the carpet. Scorching his pads. More linked than this little gold chain I once wore.

My necklace. Gone. When it happened. At the park. I lost it. Must've. The one with my name. The one I never took off. Don't even have it any more because I'm a stupid dumb fucking loser. The necklace. SONNY GAVE ME. Not Billy Speed.

Nobody else even came to my birthday. THEY WERE ALL INVITED. We had a clown, only Sonny there to help me blow out my cake.

My father grabbed him. "Tell us where you got that necklace?"

Sonny burst from my father's arms. "You can't make me," he laughed, his voice box grinding out the words.

They made him stay in his room. Every night, they went up there. Threatened. Screamed at him to confess. He refused. Just stayed in his room. Rode his bed. He didn't care.

HE DIDN'T EVEN CARE.

This Dumpster held me up. That made me happy because without it I'd be lying on the street. And I thought I *am* lying on the street. And my head fell forward and banged the Dumpster. Then banged and banged and banged and banged. The cold metal tore my skin.

When Baba ran away, she left my mother with some people. These people became my mother's parents. But my mother never forgot her real mother. As she grew up, she watched my grandmother run through our city. Screaming and howling the neighbours awake.

Years flew by. Days and nights crashed together. Streets ran on and on forever like they ran all the way to the edge of the world. No matter how far she ran, she couldn't escape the picture inside her of a girl with eyes so empty you could hide inside them.

Afraid she'd fall into the hole between her legs, Baba kept it filled up. She stayed in the scummy part of our city. Whenever we drove through, my parents yelled at us to lock the doors. She used back lanes and flop houses to fuck in, the air thick with the stench of sewers so foul it made rats scramble.

One day, prowling through these streets, Baba spied the beautiful chest of a boy splayed open, his heart beating under the black shadow of a spreading tree. The boy was small, his arms long and bony like the featherless wings of a bird. Baba scooped up the boy and hid him underneath the crumbling pavement. She yanked out one of her own teeth, filed it against a rock until it became a needle, and sewed up the boy's wound with strands of her hair. When the boy got strong enough, he reached up with his mouth and sucked on Baba's nipple until something came out. The boy and Baba grew together like something that grew out of her, leaning against buildings, begging for money with all the other beggars, change chinking into tin cups.

The boy loved Baba so hard, it tore him in half. He promised to take care of her as long as she no longer fucked, but she watched him while he fucked his way into their room and board. He walked her outside without her panties, leading her around by a leash visible only to him. He liked to imagine the wind blowing, the flesh pouting between her legs.

For a long time nothing happened. Then one day a man approached the boy — fat, with hairless legs sticking out of his shorts and buttons popping on his shirt revealing a navel as wide and deep as a crater. The boy signalled Baba, lifting his eyes above the man's bald head, then disappearing with baldie down a narrow alley.

The boy was a blade. He switched down on his haunches and unzipped the fly of the man and jacked him off. He put his mouth around the man's bullet-sized cock, puckering his lips back and forth. My grandmother spied this scene from behind a trashcan. She looked at the boy's rib bones and the elegant bone that held his shoulders together his and his and his. In that moment, her love for the boy pressed so deep it pushed her down until she dove into thick blackness. She leapt out and into the streets. Her body became packed with a feeling so intense, the only way she could release it was by fucking.

On Saturday nights, the boy wanted to go out on the town. He'd meet Baba in front of the movie theatre.

One Saturday, she was late. She never told the boy she was blowing gummy old men in the back of the beauty parlour while their wives got their hair permed. The boy ran through the streets screaming Baba's name. When he came across a long line of old men squawking like a cock fight, he stopped and parted the crowd to see Baba hanging over one old prick like a wild dark bridge.

Hearing the boy's sobs, Baba rose, her lips bruised and dripping something white. Her face twisted in the black centres of the boy's eyes. She dropped, pushing between legs, and ran. The boy ran after her. Caught her by the tail. She wriggled away, but he pelted her with gravel. A stone bit her neck. She covered her face with her hands. Her tears crackled like fires, glass crashed, the shards flew inward like tiny spears, burning down everything. The boy took the sharpest edge and sliced through several layers of skin, his body and fists shaking, the shard of glass cracking on hard linoleum tile streaked with his blood.

But that was later.

I leaned against the Dumpster, bleeding and shaking in the snow. A man came up. Picked me out of the ice. Flapped me over his shoulder. Lugged me through the snow.

"There must be a doctor on this bus," I screamed. Voices called out windows for me to shut up. I screamed anyway. The man carried me down the lane past tall skinny buildings, iron ladders running up and down their backs like zippers.

The man carried me inside. Put me on a big bed. Took off my shoes and pants.

"Please, please," I cried. "If you cut anything off, I want it done at the hospital."

The man told me to hold still.

"Do you think I'll have to get my leg amputated?" I knew about gangrene. I didn't want to hobble around on sticks.

I felt him go over my leg, carefully, like a doctor. "I can't tell that yet," he said. "Don't think so."

He fluffed extra blankets on me, tucking them into the mattress. "I made up the bed," he said. "I wasn't expecting company, but I do it everyday for myself."

I opened my eyes. Sunlight. Morning.

I lay on his big bed. The room was big and clean and white like the moon. New paint smell. Nothing in there except this bed — a big square with white sheets like the kind people fuck on in movies that scared me for some reason — and a flowered shower curtain hung up for a door. The curtain led into a little kitchenette, I saw, as the man pulled it back, calling out, "We've got tea, we've got coffee, we've got water."

The curtain parted. The voice belonged to a face I'd seen before. The creepy man. The man from the bar. He smiled like he knew me. Something zinged up my stomach and my heart froze.

I wanted to run away. I couldn't move.

Lance.

Lance brought me a styrofoam cup, a string dangling down one side. He sat cross-legged, cowboy boot tips pointing out, dipped the bag in the water, and blew on a plastic spoon.

"I've got to go," I told him, getting up.

He pushed me back down. "It's too dangerous."

"No," I said. "It's just — I don't like owing anything. It's not my style, or whatever."

"Are we or are we not officially friends?"

"I guess."

"Then just hang out until this blizzard's over."

I realized, I might be onto a good thing with Lance. He wasn't like my boyfriend. We read magazines. Ate burritos. Donuts with jam inside. I know what you're thinking. But he wasn't like that. He had this way of looking — like we'd been friends a long time.

And, anyway, he wasn't at all the way you think. So we sat there. And sat there. He got up and yanked open the black curtains. Two bricks for propping the window sat on the sill. Snow banged and foamed against the windows. We were on the ocean. And I knew Lance really liked me. You could tell the way he turned around and smiled at me when he opened the curtains. My head swirled like the snow. A few flakes stuck to the pane and held on until the wind pulled them away.

"Hey," Lance said. "Look at the crow."

A baby crow had landed on the ledge, battered around with the wind. Its twig feet clenched the ledge, rocking back and forth.

"I don't know if it thinks it's looking at itself or another crow, but it looks sad," I said.

He walked right up to the window and stared at the crow's face. "How does the crow look sad?"

The crow trembled, peering at its reflection against the thick black curtain.

"Well, it doesn't open its mouth or peep or anything," I said. "It just stares straight at itself in the window."

"Boo hoo," he laughed. "Dumb crow doesn't even have the brains to fly south."

We both stood and watched. Every so often, Lance tapped on the window with his finger. The crow never moved. Budged. Flinched.

I asked him to stop.

"Don't you want a pet?" he said. "Come on, everyone wants a pet. When I was a kid that's all I ever thought of, getting a little dog or cat."

He grunted open the window. Snow gushed in. He yanked the window back down with both hands. The bird didn't move.

I whispered at him not to touch it. "It won't be able to go back to its natural habitat."

"Sure it will."

"It can't. Everyone knows that. It'll get a human smell on it, and then it will be a freak and all the other birds will kill it. Don't touch him."

I danced around Lance.

He made a cage with his hands. Lifted the bird into the apartment. Nudged the window shut with his elbow.

The bird squawked, its eyes bursting needle points.

"The bird's just fine. Aren't you, big fella? See, he's happy. He was lonely out there."

It twitched. Twitched harder. Lance's mouth was big, laughing and excited as he carried the bird around the apartment. "I like crow," he said. "Chicken of the tree."

"Don't say that," I said. "Crows are like people."

"They aren't like people," he said softly, speaking to the crow. "Crows have a very different psyche than people as a matter of fact. They've got a crow consciousness."

"You're going to kill it," I said.

The crow smashed against the window. Lance managed to reach out and grab it, holding onto the wings with both hands.

"It doesn't look dead to me," he said. The wing muscles vibrated wildly, the beak pointed and squawked. "Look. I'm just protecting it."

"You might as well kill it," I cried. "The other birds will do it." I covered my face with my hands. "It will be horrible."

"No it won't," he said.

"Now you'll have to keep it," I said. "And if you move to another city you'll have to take it with you."

"No way," he said, dropping the crow on the bed. The bird flapped against the walls, screeching and cawing.

"You'll have to give it a name and make it a pet."

He turned to me. "Keep it down. I can't think when I hear voices bouncing off the walls. It's obscene."

"You raised your voice."

"PLEASE. DO NOT get into that nibbly nabbly bullshit," he said. He stepped in little circles, refusing to look at me. "I hate that shit. It makes me sick. What are we, a pair of schoolgirls?"

The crow skittered against the wall. Lance bent over, fingering it, smoothing its feathers with his hand. The crow's head darted around the room, eyes staring, beak pointing.

"You've just killed a crow," I whispered.

He smoothed the crow's feathers. The crow squawked. "Nobody's killing nobody," Lance said. He stroked the crow's feathers, at first soft, then harder. The crow squawked louder and louder. Lance kept fingering the bird. Pressing its neck. The bird shrieked. Its head vibrated. Then went still.

I shrugged into a crease in the wall.

Lance just stood there, like he was thinking of what to say.

"I guess we won't have to worry about the crow no more."

He opened the window and flung the crow out.

I ran to the window. A black lump lay in the snow. The snow blew over the lump. It blew and blew until I felt like blowing my brains out.

We didn't say anything for a long time. Then I couldn't sit still. I paced up and down.

"If you just calm down, everything will be okay," he said.

I told him I didn't want to calm down. I picked up a brick from the sill and hurled it through the window, making a jagged, sharp hole.

Lance swung around. His eyes flashed all over me.

He scrunched up a piece of newspaper and stuffed it in the hole.

"That's very mature." He stared at me like he was trying to figure me out. "What did I ever do to you?"

For a few minutes I didn't feel anything except my legs walking towards my parka. Lance looked at me like nothing happened, then lassoed me with his arm like he was trying to be cute.

"Where do you think you're going?" he said.

"I have to be someplace."

"That's too bad," he said. "We were having fun." Then he said, very casually, "Why not just skip it?"

"It's my psychiatrist." My voice shook, the words sticking inside my mouth. "If you don't go they charge you a hundred bucks."

He held my shoulders and walked me away from the door.

He said, "Tell me what the problem is."

"You killed it," I told him.

He stood there, looking at the floor, then raised his eyes.

"I don't get it," he said.

"The bird is dead," I sobbed into my hands.

"I see. Because I killed a bird — by accident, for Christ's sake — I am now a murderer."

I just stared at him.

"I'd like to interject here," he said. "I've never hurt or inflicted pain on anyone. I happen to be incapable of it."

I told him I had to leave.

"You're blowing this out of proportion," he shouted.

I took a few steps, then ran for the door, but Lance jumped in front of it, his boots striking the floor like gunshots. "I swear. Listen to me," he begged. "Please. Everything is okay."

"What are you going to do? Kidnap me?" It sounded so dumb, I laughed.

Lance's neck jerked. "What do you mean? Is that what you're going to tell them?"

I didn't know what he meant.

"Your parents?" he screamed. "The police? You can't tell people anything happened," he told me. "Because it didn't."

"You said I could leave when I want to." I kept looking at the door, figuring out my escape. My parka was slipping from my hands. Maybe he'd been to jail. Maybe he'd killed a person.

His eyes were as sharp as the sun on the snow. I looked away.

"I'm never going to see my parents."

He punched the air with his fist. I jumped. "Everyone says that. But they don't mean it."

"I mean it."

"I made a mistake," he pleaded with me. He climbed down to his knees, head level with mine. "Isn't it possible for a person to make a mistake? Is it against the fucking law? Are you going to tell people something happened here? Because it didn't."

I didn't say a thing.

He got up. Scrunched his face. "You can't go out there," he said, running his fingers through his hair. "It's insane." Then he turned to me, "Of course, you've worked out what to do about the blizzard. Food. Shelter. How to handle the lunatics. Frostbite. AIDS. You must have worked all that out, right?"

The phone rang.

It rang again.

And again.

"Aren't you going to answer?" I said.

It rang again.

He walked over. Kicked the phone.

"You can't leave here thinking something happened," he said. He turned around and stared out the window. "Look, I'm really sorry about the bird," he said. "It was an accident, okay? It was a fucking accident. It must've been scared and had a fucking heart attack or something."

"You're a liar." I almost whispered it. "You're a rotten fucking liar."

"I guess we'll have to agree to disagree," he said, "because I had no intention of killing anything." He sat down. Rubbed his face with his hands and smiled up. "Once the blizzard's over, we can go to the petting zoo."

"I don't want to go to the petting zoo."

"How could you not? They've got little animals. Babies. You can fit them in your hand. Then we can go to a restaurant. We can eat steaks. What's your favourite restaurant?"

"I'm not hungry," I told him.

He wouldn't let it go. "What's your favourite restaurant?"

"I don't have one."

"Everyone's got a favourite."

I told him the Pony Corral.

"We'll go there."

"It moved. I don't even know where it is any more."

I kept looking at the door. He walked around and around on the floor like he was trying to figure it out. "Why don't you just stab me?" he said. "I was just trying to do something nice." He walked to the door and swung it open.

"You want me to leave now?"

He stood there, glooming down. "You wore me down. I'm drained."

I didn't move. I don't know why. I just didn't.

"If you wanna go, then go. Think what you want about me."

The wind banged and howled against the window.

Lance looked at the door like he didn't care if I stayed.

I looked at Lance.

His face was blotched. His tongue ran over and over his teeth. Black crow. Snow.

The window glass banged faster and harder than my heart.

I looked at Lance again. He smiled. His mouth creeped into a little smirk I hadn't noticed before. Made his eyes crinkle.

Black crow. Snow.

The wind shrieked between trees. Made me jump.

Lance.

Black crow. Snow.

Lance.

The way he smirked made his eyes nice. Wriggling away.

Smirking in my mother's lap. The lights, the snow. Lance glittered between my lashes, his long hair, his beard, his sad face like a librarian or Jesus, like Jesus on the cross.

"What are you still doing here?" he shouted at me.

I didn't move.

Because I had to stay.

"I want to," I said.

"What?"

"Stay." My voice quavered. "I really want to."

Then I asked Lance to sit down, just to sit down. I kept on talking and then we fell to the floor just like that.

The room got darker.

Cars flashed back and forth.

"You can stay," Lance said. "It's your prerogative."

"I know that."

"As long as you know. As long as you understand the situation. It's nothing to me."

"I know," I said.

"We'll get a new bird to replace the one that died. One that's used to being inside. Some kind of parrot."

I started thinking Lance's killing the bird must've been an accident, otherwise what would he want with a new bird. And so I started thinking maybe, maybe I could stay. And it reminded me of a long, long time ago. So long ago I can hardly remember.

"We'll take a plane," he said. "Once we get there everything will be okay. I had this car, but I totalled it." He took a creased up picture from his pocket. There were people, standing in front of a hamburger stand. The sun burst in their faces like a sunflower. Water ran behind the people. "The water's blue like that all year round. I hope you won't mind flipping hamburgers."

"I can't see the colour of the water anyway," I told him. "Besides, I've got this boyfriend." And I started thinking maybe maybe maybe I can go with Lance. I started getting all sad just thinking about it because Lance wasn't my prince. And I'm not really a princess.

"We got to get plane tickets," he said. "Good food, and they serve it to you on real plates, and we don't need to worry about the money." He was pacing now. "I've got friends."

"What about your apartment?" I said, looking around.

"Fuck all that," he said. "I've got a really good feeling about this."

His fingertips brushed my eyelid.

And I thought maybe I could do this.

"Everything's gonna be alright," he said. Just like in the song. Then he sang it. And I believed him. And he rocked me and said, "As soon as this blizzard's over we'll go have one of those dollar ninety-nine breakfasts and draw a plan of attack." And he had these ideas. All these ideas I can't even remember now, but they seemed good, like they could really happen.

We lay on the floor like that a long time.

And I was going on a plane. For the first time.

His fingers touched my hair, like he wasn't sure what he wanted to do. His mouth blurring my cheek and my ear. This close. I actually felt something. It wasn't like with my boyfriend, but it was like when you want to hold onto something warm. That must be a kind of love and anyway his eyes got black and shadowy like backlanes, and I wanted to sit inside them so nobody could catch me.

The door banged. The knob squeaked back and forth.

Lance scrambled up. Leaned against the door. "Who's there?"

"Me," a man called.

Lance spun, head jerking around the room like the crow's eyes. "Fuck. Jesus." He made a jagged motion with his hand, hissing for me to get behind the shower curtain.

"What's going on?" I whispered back.

"I don't know."

I heard a key stick into the hole. It didn't click into place. The knob jangled wildly. Fists banged on the door.

"Open up."

"Why?" said Lance.

"You know why. Let's have it."

"You should have called ahead," Lance said to the door in a soft little voice. "There's a law against just showing up."

The voice on the other side of the door boomed, "Don't talk to me about the law, you fuck."

"I'm not dressed," Lance called. He leaned against the door and said, "I'll be right down."

"When?"

Lance told him half an hour.

"Open up. Open up now."

Lance didn't say anything.

"I'll kick it in."

Lance blinked and pulled at his face. I heard quick steps skim the floor. A body threw itself against the door. Clomped back. Threw itself against the door over and over. The door shuddered. Exploded. A big fat man grunted into the wall — the biggest fattest man I've seen.

"Be cool, man," Lance said.

"I don't want to be cool," said the man. "Have you forgotten about our deal?"

Lance lit a cigarette. The match snapped. Lance's voice shook. "It was very dry out there."

"What are you saying?" said the fat man.

"I'm saying I don't have it. I'll get it tomorrow."

"Fuck that. You owe me. First you said you had this big deal. And this big other deal."

"I know. I'm sorry."

"Fuck sorry."

"What do you want from me?" Lance's eyes flicked with fear.

"I want what you owe me. Give me my money. I'm not leaving without it." The fat man banged his fist hard against the wall.

I fell to the tile. Dragged myself on my stomach like a bug to the shower curtain and peered out.

I saw the feet of the bed. The feet of the men. Lance rocking back and forth. The big fat man steady.

Lance whispered something to the man I couldn't hear.

"Fuck you," the fat man said.

I got up and opened a can of pork and beans. The rusty opener wouldn't bite. I kept opening and closing its teeth, cranking the handle until the lid sunk in. Just then, a bang.

I peered behind the curtain. Lance leaned against the wall, holding his stomach. The fat man whacked Lance across the mouth with an open hand. Lance blinked like he didn't believe it. The man threw Lance backwards onto the floor. Lance fell and crumpled, struggled forward, swinging his fists, but the fat man pulled Lance's hair back, punching him in the face. Lance curled up in a corner, hugging himself like he didn't have a skeleton. Drops of blood spattered the wall.

The man kicked and kicked Lance with his boots, until I saw Lance's mouth barely move. The man leaned over, ear cocked. Lance said something I couldn't hear. The man stared at him, then at the curtain. Then clomped to the shower curtain and yanked it from me. The man stood there, looking at me with blank eyes. A tongue wormed its way between the folds of his skin.

"It's gonna be okay," he said. He stretched his big fat arms towards me. "Come to Daddy. That's a girl. Nice and easy."

The man backed up towards the bed, unbuttoning his shirt with one hand. Sat on the bed's edge, a big hairy stomach flapped onto his thighs, big-nippled breasts dangling. He pushed his wire glasses back on his sweaty nose, wiped the sweat off his forehead with his fat arm. Gestured at me to come close. Lance had conked out. A zoo smell climbed up from the floor.

I stood there, finger stuck in the can of beans.

The fat man got up. Came at me. Shit, shit, shit. I wasn't that little bitch with no tits. It would stuff Its finger up Its nose. It would analyse, think, assess, and crunch the facts. But I'm not It. I'm not It. I'm not It.

A mountain of fat blubbered in front of me. Skin shone where the stomach pushed out.

I dropped to the floor. Crawled around. His fat hands grabbed my waist, yanked me up, ripped my clothes off like a chocolate wrapper.

He stepped back to look. His tongue squirmed out. Flicked across his blubbery lips.

I stood up, shower curtain swirling my ankles. He unbuckled his belt, whipped his clanking belt from the loops, and cracked the air like a lion tamer.

"Don't make me hurt you," he said.

"I'll just scream," I said, my hair tangling in my mouth. "Somebody will call the police. The police will call my parents."

"Nobody's calling anybody," he said.

I screamed like a maniac.

He yelled, "shut up you crazy bitch, shut up you crazy bitch, shut up you crazy bitch."

I lowered my head like a dog.

"What are you doing?" he said.

I stuck out my tongue. Slackened my jaw. Shook my head. Made out I was spaz or mental. "I'm going to puke."

He told me to go ahead and puke.

"No. I need air. I'm having an attack."

I stuck my fingers down my throat. Coughed. Nothing happened.

The man laughed. His dirty fingers crept lower and lower.

He edged towards me. A wet ball dripped from his dirty mouth. Something glowed in that ball. Caught inside.

Sonny's face swelling and shrinking. I started to panic, cry. I couldn't stop. I COULDN'T EVEN STOP.

And I remembered this thing. I remembered this thing when I was lonely and scared and had no one to talk to. Because of the night. Because the only sound were their lungs beating away in the other room. So what I did was, I crawled over the bars of Sonny's crib. I crawled up next to Sonny. And he was soft and warm. His breath the only thing burring against my neck.

I was scared to touch the ball of wet, afraid it might break, Sonny might fall out or disappear.

The fat man moaned at my ear, inside me. His zipper whined. He squeezed my shoulders with his hands, pushing me down to the shower curtain. I reached up to push him away. Pushed hard against his face, harder, my hand slipping from eye to chin.

The fat man grabbed his face with his hands, staggering back, pants fell, tangling his ankles as he hobbled and hopped around the room, skin dangling between his legs like a turkey chinstrap, a thatch of hair, cowboy boots tapping the floor. He pulled his hand back, and blood gushed out. He squirmed and held his face together — my hand, hot, the tin can lid glinting — as I ran for the door.

Flights and flights of stairs, elevator busted, everything so sad and fucked up. Through the front door, I ran and ran and ran naked down the street, the shower curtain flapping behind me, a car honked, my legs springing across the snow, arms twirling at my sides like windmill blades, blood sliding from my hands and wrists.

My name is Tracey Berkowitz.
Tracey Zerowitz. Forty below Zerowitz.

Crows burst the sky. They shrieked and dove behind me. I raised my arms around my head and fell to my knees.

I wanted a bomb to explode me. I wanted Hiroshima. I wanted Molotov flower baskets. I wanted giant metal shards cutting the world.

I raced between buildings, all the way to Blue Jay Park. The birds screamed like maniacs, like ten thousand tiny holes filling the sky. I stood beside the river. The moon sparked the black, the snow, flickering like eyes, a trillion tiny eyes. I stepped on them to make them go away. As soon as my foot budged, they came back. Eyes everywhere, flickering with the moon.

My foot slipped. I slid down a hole. Deep. I spun around and around, falling, the whole world swirling into the hole with me.

In our city, my grandmother became famous. Men tricked her into sex. Over and over. She wasn't dumb. She just liked to pretend. All she gave a shit about was that the men loved her. But they didn't love her because she didn't let them see past her dumb sad clown mask. Underneath the mask was just a hole anyway.

All she talked about were the men on horseback, hoofs pounding up through the grass, dust whipping up under the hoofs, whipping, rising, clouding the men into ghosts. Every night, she waited for the horsemen. They split her in two. Between the starlight and the restless nights. She paced curbs. Chased cars filled with boys and men through the streets. A chance to turn back the clocks in her head. They just slowed their motors, pointing, honking, and laughing alongside her. "Over here, baby." She stretched her hands far out, veering too close to the wheels of their cars until they either got too bored or too scared of their game and zoomed past her. She twirled and twirled through the streets until some man with a bad smell and a scratchy beard caught her in his hand like a top. She'd follow the man to a hotel. Each night, she squeezed her eyes closed as the stranger strode on top of her, riding her into the night like a supermarket pony. Each day she woke up in an empty room, the light dazzling her eyes wide open like from an operation, looking at the bed beside her, the man gone. Toothless in a tattered dress, she searched the streets, swearing she'd kill him kill him kill him. Went up to strangers, asking where's the horseman? People rolled their eyes, having no clue who she was asking for. On good days, she'd tell them about her daughter and her daughter's family. They live in a good home and they love her very very much, telling them how they'd pick her up in their station wagon and she'd stay all day, play with the grandchildren and feed them her cakes. People just walked past or nodded and smiled her away. She didn't notice, just kept stumbling and twirling.

Here is the rest of the girl with no tits.

So, this week, Sonny and me smuggled out. This one time. Where? Where the sky splits from the world.

It wasn't my fault. Grounded in that house. I hated it. I knew I was bored. BORED. It made me crazy. And winter. And below zero.

They sat in the family room. Watching the weather channel. Watching the record highs, the lows, the frostbite warnings, the windchill factors. It was the only time they did anything together.

I stood there, holding my parka. My mother looked at my father. She closed her eyes.

"There's a blizzard," my father said, nodding at the TV.

"Can't I go out for a minute?" I said. "I need to relax."

"Forget it," she said very fast and very hard.

At the very same time, he said, "You are grounded."

"What am I supposed to do?" I said.

My father leaned over. "You are going to lock the door and watch your brother."

Sliding against the wall, I glared at them.

"I might as well kill myself," I said.

"Snap out of it," he warned.

"I can't do this," my mother shrieked.

"Look at Mommy. Look at what you are doing to Mommy," my father said. "Promise us you'll stay inside."

"I promise," I said very fast.

"Mommy and I love you. Don't you know that?"

I looked at her on the couch. It wasn't love I saw.

Went to the door. Put on my parka. Silent like the snow. Clicked on the door, slow and careful like a cat burglar.

"Are you locking the door?"

"Yes," I said, slipping out.

"Good girl," I heard him call out.

I turned to run. Sonny stood there in the snow. "There's a blizzard starting," I told him.

He smirked. I was about to yell at him to go back inside.

I hated them. I knew they'd kill me. Fuck them, I thought. I DIDN'T EVEN CARE.

Miles of bungalows. Cow heads sitting in the snow like Easter Island. Winter stripping the trees naked.

If you don't run in a straight line, bullets can't get you.

Sonny and I crisscrossed the field. We ran and ran to Blue Jay Park. Over the little banks of snow, rippling under our feet. Mouths wide open to the sky. Snow like daydreams flying in.

Sonny heaved a bark out. Threw it across the open field. Punctured the sky with it. Our feet plunged into snow, almost to grass, wet and matted down like the hair of birds cracking out of eggs. Each other's footprints, every step a landmine exploding.

If you walk all the way to the edge, you get to Texas. If you walk past Texas, you get to the sun. If you dig all the way through the earth, you get to China.

What would the Chinese think, our heads shooting up through the mud? There are too many Chinese. We'd fix our eyes into slits, learn Chinese, eat rice. Nobody'd ever catch us.

People go to the park even when it's cold enough to freeze your nips. Even when your car won't start. Burning tips of cigarettes. Bushes rustling. Foaming tailpipes of dark cars, shadows moving in them.

I didn't talk to Sonny, hoping someone would show up. He ran around and around. Climbed the trees. Crashed and exploded. I kept wishing I didn't have a brother.

I heard something swish.

IT WASN'T MY FUCKING FAULT. Sonny should never have followed me. You couldn't control him.

Sonny did anything JUST TO SEE WHAT WOULD HAPPEN. Even if I dragged him down the street by the leash off my tartan skirt, throwing pieces of last night's roast beef, he'd eat off the sidewalk. Once, coming home from Myra Bernie's, I heard wheels spinning behind me. His raspy laugh. He'd stolen my bike. Legs stretching for the pedals. Flicking. Disappearing out my eye corners. I pretended I didn't notice. When I finally looked back, Sonny was gone.

I shouldn't have told you anything. I go on these little vacations in my head. It's like my one friend I ever had. Myra Bernie — not any more because her mother said Tracey's dysfunctional — she went on these vacations with her family to England. When she came back she said, "I went to England." And I said, "I went to England, too." Only I'd never been there, right? I'd never been farther than Bemiji in a motel. So she said to me, "You've never been to England." And I said, "Sure I have." And she called me a liar and I said, "I've been there in my mind." And I had.

Sonny's the air and the trees and the snow. He's everywhere.

Sonny jumped from the trees. Landed in the snow. Pretended he was a bomb. I yelled Shut up. I didn't even want to yell shut up. I just wanted to pretend for one second he didn't exist. And I looked around and wondered where were all the kids. The ones in the bushes. In cars. Fucking. Shooting up. Next day, people whispering about what those park kids did — as if they were actually there in the park with them. Only they weren't.
    And I didn't even care what they'd do to me.
    I DIDN'T EVEN CARE.

But nobody showed up.

And I swore at the top of my lungs — but silent, here deep inside me — God do you hate me that much? Why is my life so boring?

And in my head came this saying I heard once on a TV infomercial: only boring people get bored. And I couldn't get this idea out of my head. Only boring people get bored. Only boring people get bored, like an extended dance track that kept scratching and repeating, scratching, and then I saw It, the girl with no tits.

It stood there, the girl with no tits. It was asking for it. It never should have been there in the first place.

It's not my fault. IT WAS THE GIRL'S FAULT.

"Come on," Sonny yelled. "Hypnotize me again." Twirl. Bark. Run. Twirl. Bark. Stop. Run. Run. Run. He barked, down on all fours, twirling away on the river ice. Like he believed me.

Billy Speed must've been there the whole time. I didn't notice at first. He leaned against his car that's three colours of rust — red, brown, green — trembling, exhaust foaming out. He looked at the trees and the sky. I didn't even know Billy Speed liked the trees and the sky. HOW WAS I SUPPOSED TO KNOW SOMETHING LIKE THAT?

The girl with no tits saw Billy Speed and stopped. He leaned against the car. The girl stared down.

"Come here, so I can talk to you," he called to It.

What It said had to be perfect. PERFECT. It will make a tapestry of words. He will see a thousand pictures in one of Its words. A thousand words equals millions of pictures. A million pictures will be a galaxy to Billy Speed. Billy Speed will see stars. The girl with no tits will become Billy Speed's star.

BUT IT COULDN'T THINK OF ANYTHING TO SAY. It knew ideas didn't pump from Its brain like a hotspring. Even the brilliant need time to be creative. Think of Einstein. He came up with the Theory of Relativity while asleep. The girl knew if It were asleep It would be amazing.

"I should leave," It said.

"Well — see you," he said. Smirking, but looking away.

The snow blew over and over their footprints.

Nobody will ever know they were here. Somebody had to remember. The way their feet muffled through the snow. The way the branches curved over their heads. The way the snow clumped on his car like wedding-flower Kleenexes. The way the snow floated and swirled, making everything — even It — beautiful.

Far away, the girl heard barking and pants whisking on the ice.

"I can't talk to you from over there," he said. "Do you need a ride?"

"I should leave," It said.

"Well — see you."

It didn't move. IT DIDN'T EVEN MOVE.

He talked to It. Billy Speed actually talked to the girl with no tits, like he was interested and serious, his forehead pleating like my tartan skirt.

"You're in my class, right?" He said Its name. Its name. And the girl with no tits thought, he actually knows my name.

It didn't say anything.

"We can go someplace."

"I can't."

It's so stupid I could murder It. He wanted to go someplace with It. He wanted to be seen with It. Someplace.

"Where would we go?" It asked.

"Drive around," he said.

It stood in the snow like a faun caught in the flame of a match. Looked at Its own feet. Looked at his feet. No boy ever offered to drive It anywhere before, except to piano and dance classes. And It couldn't believe it. It just couldn't believe he was here in front of It. It noticed the snow flaking and blowing and just now It heard the sound of pants whisking on the ice — the barking had stopped — and It probably looked away like It forgot something.

"You'd better get home," It said, saying the words fast. Too fast. "Saw it on TV. Blizzard. Eight-foot snow drifts predicted. Windchill factor. Frostbite warning. Maybe we won't have to go to school. Not that I would anyway." And It laughed. Too hard.

He looked like he didn't care about the blizzard. Like he wanted to lead It somewhere. Like he knew It would go anywhere. Like he didn't even have to ask.

It went towards the car. Step. Step. Step. That horrible stringer of snot. That piece of phlegm I coughed up.

It stared down at his feet. Became obsessed with the footprints. Its footprints. Next to his. Its expensive prints of the boots with the square heels. It hoped he'd notice they're the boots EVERYONE wears. His footprints. Runners. Too cold for runners. He had no money for boots. He was from a poor family. The most perfect runners in the world. Left perfect cuts in the snow. The girl wanted to pick his footprints up and save them, but it was the kind of snow that doesn't last. The kind that blows away.

It kept saying It should go.

He leaned over and swung the door open. Wide open.

Sonny softly barking Its name.

He looked at the door. At the girl. He looked up. Drew It towards him by an invisible leash. Into the car. Into the front seat. Vinyl and torn. A giant slash with stuff poking out. Still, a dream. Beautiful and perfect. Falling, falling. And It wanted to make it last, slowly, crawling into the hole of the car on her knees, him following and pulling the door shut behind them.

It sat there. In Billy Speed's car. Whose license plate It memorized: JKF 826 — a license plate easy to remember because it was like JFK. It wondered if he ever thought about that. If they ever had the same thought once, about the license plate initials.

They sat in the same car. The space between him and her shrunk. Shrunk to zero.

Bees die after they fuck. Flies spark and die.

Their lips stuck together. "You know what to do," he told It. He took Its hand with his hand and pressed It down. Where he pressed was hard and It felt something move under there. MOVE. A small animal. A hamster. It bit Its fingers. Giggled. "Do something," he said. "Creative."

It looked up at him.

His mouth tightened and he pulled back to the edge of the torn seat like he was mad.

He squinted like he was trying to figure the girl with no tits out. He didn't even kiss It. Then he did it. Pressed his tongue between Its lips. Then said just relax. Just relax. Just relax.

The girl felt his thighs press against Its. His bony shoulders. Their breath steaming the windows white. The heat whirring.

He took Its hand. Where he ended and It began was a blur. Better than a rock video. The whole world went on pause. He reached for Its face. Its mouth. His fingers touched Its body.

ITS BODY.

I could've gotten sick.

I was sick.

It didn't stop.

It didn't even think.

Its body climbed into that car with Billy Speed.

Sonny calling me back.

Shouting my name the whole time.

But It was afraid to say something. Afraid to make him mad. And soon Sonny's voice tangled with the wind in the trees.

Then It heard something. Sticks. Glass breaking. Something. But It didn't stop. It didn't stop, tightening up Its leg and his leg tightened against Its and — It could've pushed him away and smashed the door open; It could've burned a cigarette into his face until the flesh got black, curled, and separated like newspaper pages — but before It knew, he pushed It back on the vinyl seat and crawled in.

Its hole.

The whole of It.

He fit inside.

Its eyes were open, but Its mind froze shut. Heat whirred. Its body shook almost in half. It didn't hear Itself crying on that torn vinyl car seat, but water was sliding from Its eyes into Its ears, nose, mouth, everywhere, everywhere, everywhere. He cried out, started shaking, his hair tumbling and swinging over his face. It reached up to his face with Its hand, but he jerked his face away.

He sat up, straightened himself behind the steering wheel. Did up his pants. It sat up on Its side. Its leg inches from his leg.

Blood smeared on Its thigh.

Its own blood.

Its hole blood.

They sat in his car. He held his cigarette between two fingers like a movie star, his hair long and jungling. His arm stretched across It like a roller coaster safety bar — It shivered — but his arm didn't in any way touch It. He yanked the handle. The door jammed. His shoulder rammed and banged the door open.

"Well — see you," he said.

Bye Billy Speed Bye Billy Speed Bye Billy Speed.

It stepped out of the car.

I stepped out of the car.

I fell down.

Billy Speed ground his wheels into the snow and drove away, the trees and the sky floating across his face. I touched the cuts his tires made in the snow and pushed into them with my fingers.

I stood up. Felt around my neck. The necklace with my name wasn't there any more. Must've torn.

Sonny.

I forgot.

One day, the cakes stopped coming to our house. Baba got too old to bring them on the bus. She got Smelly. Peed her bed. Shrunk. Her bones crumbled to windowsill dust.

Baba parted the dust, rising from the tips of whips and horsebeats. Soared around like a dream. Fell down hot curvy mouths. Red tears jewelling up and dropping in wild mud. Angels circled stained blood roofs. Crashed down on our heads like fiery birds.

Didn't want to go. My mother made me.

We stood there in the hospital, staring down at my grandmother. Three generations caught inside each other like Russian dolls.

"I swallowed the sun." That's the last thing my grandmother said.

Down the halls of the hospital we heard her screams. Nobody wanted to go in there to see that mouth open and close when the words came out. Baba slept through a day, so all she saw were two moons. Because she missed the sun, she was sure it had fallen into her mouth. Her mouth gaped open, deep down like a dark bag, a puckered string for a mouth that pulled tight when she took her last breath, before the hospital wrapped her in a white sheet and put her away.

After my mother saw her mother, she stopped planting flowers. She didn't want to fill those holes with her flowers any more.

At the end of the day, the sun swells, its pointed tips touching the edge of the world. My grandmother ran for the edge of the world so far she swallowed a piece of the sun. It glowed inside her until it burst, and the flames flew from her mouth.

I ran through the park, calling Sonny, Sonny, Sonny. Calling his name over and over until my lungs hurt. The streets ran on and on forever like they don't ever end. They ran all the way to the edge of the world to this big empty hole inside me.

One day you fall for this boy. In the middle of nowhere. In the middle of snow. He touches your body with his fingers. He burns holes in your skin with his mouth. And it hurts when you look at him. And it hurts when you don't. And it feels like someone cuts you open with a jagged piece of glass. And then you realize you always felt that way.

I can't stop these tears from burning my eyes.

I can't stop tearing my skin apart.

I can't stop tearing my eyes out.

I can't grab hold of anything. Even as I grab hold of the sides of this hole everything crumbles up around me.

Nothing matters. Not even that I'm on this crummy stupid bus. Because since that girl saw that boy, everything became a fiery blur that she can't put out even if everything wet inside her comes out. Even if she turns from the hole of her inside out.

Sonny's everywhere. There's nothing you or I or anyone can do about it. We won't find Sonny. Or if we do, he'll be standing in front of some convenience store. And I told them a lie when I said he just disappeared.

My lungs burned that day in Blue Jay Park when Billy Speed left me. I ran, birds hooting, churning over my head. I just ran and ran until my legs were a rotating blur I didn't feel any more. Sonny's face dangled. I wanted to stick a needle and explode it. I ran and ran and ran all the way back home.

My parents were in the family room. They looked up.

They can't know. They can't ever know. We looked all over. For two days, he never came back. I slunk through the house. Concentrated really hard to disappear. That's what I did before I ran away.

Back down in the hole, I opened my mouth. A scream slithered up through my throat and ran through the snow. I crawled up from my hole. Ran down the street in this shower curtain. On the corner stood a group of boys. And Billy Speed. The boys laughed. Threw snowballs at me. Yelled, "There It goes."

I ran, my shower curtain blowing out around me, wrapping around my ankles. "Not Billy Speed," I screamed. "He wouldn't laugh at me. He wouldn't laugh at me. He wouldn't laugh at me."

He did.

I fell

like ice

breaking the world

wide open.

My name is Estuary Palomino. Palomino is the colour of the city where I'm from. I imagined the boys on horseback, rising above me by their thick, sinewy arms. Because I'm small, I roll under and away from the boys through the tall grasses, the boys rolling after me, tearing out the front of my dress, biting my nipples roughly between their teeth. The heat of the dust rises between my legs. The trembling shudders my body so hard I have to lean against a tree. I rise against the black window of this dirty bus.

Stars. They never go away. Even if you die. Even if the world explodes.

Don't sleep. We have to find him.

I can feel the floor of this bus under my feet.

I can feel the engine vibrating under the floor.

I can feel the wheels spinning over the pavement.

I can cross the pointed mountains. I can cross the blue seas. Nobody can stop me. Nobody can make me stand still.

Look outside at that big yellow sun bursting out of the world.

We're getting warmer.

ACKNOWLEDGEMENTS

Thanks to

John Sorrell, my mentor, who taught me to write and who guided this book into life.

Robert Kroetsch, who inspired me to believe this book was possible.

Martha Sharpe, my editor at Anansi, and Esta Spalding of Anansi's editorial advisory board, who made important contributions to this book.

Keith Maillard in the Department of Creative Writing at the University of British Columbia, as well as Joan MacLeod and Zsuzsi Gartner, who gave me knowledgeable support.

My family, friends, and colleagues, who offered me advice and encouragement, including Myles Blank, Frank Borg, Marnie Darnel, Daphne Gage, Victor Janoff, and Deanna Levis.

The Explorations Program of the Canada Council for the Arts, which awarded me a grant to work on this book.

Prairie Fire, in versions, and Tongue Tide — in which earlier versions of some of these fragments have appeared.

Jeremy Woolf who, through the years, has held my hand.